The Kinky Side of
of
Scrooge

CW01500490

Veronica Cane

GTQ LLC

Orlando, FL

Veronica Cane/GTQ LLC
P O Box 540375
Orlando, FL, 32854
www.gtq.com

Publisher's Note: This is a work of fiction. Names, characters, places and incidents are a product of the author's imagination. Locales and public names are sometimes used for atmospheric purposes. Any resemblance to actual people, living or dead, or to businesses, companies, events, institutions, or locales is completely coincidental.

The Kinky Side of Scrooge/Veronica Cane. -- 1st ed.
ISBN 978-1-51943639-9

CONTENTS

Perhaps he was getting too old for this. Or maybe he had just lost the capability to be thrilled by it. His last relationships had been a succession of repeated acts and actions that no longer were able to warm him within. He hadn't experienced the thrill of being with a new submissive in a long time, they all seemed to be alike, to want the same things and act the same way. Not even trying new toys, new kinks, and new devices had the power to make him feel happy.

Sometimes he was tempted to stop trying, to stop looking. The only thing that stopped him from doing so was the knowledge that going back to a vanilla world would only lead to more boredom, to more frustration and to more loneliness.

"Hi Alec, where's Adele?" His friend, James, joined him at the bar, patting his shoulder before sitting in the stall next to him.

"Hey, James. I'm fine thank you, what about you? How's everything going?" he answered in a monotone. "I would appreciate being asked that, before having my private life assaulted," he added with a self-deprecating grimace.

"Oh, yes, I'm sorry," James said, with a grin that showed he wasn't sorry at all. "So, how are you, and where's Adele?" he repeated, teasing.

Alec shook his head, amused at how beyond help his friend's behavior was.

"I'm fine, thank you, and I believe Adele should be in the loving arms of her new Dom," he answered, looking straight ahead at the countless bottles lined up behind the bar. Mark, the bartender, rushed to and fro, getting people their orders, with the help of two beautiful slaves who loved to help him.

"You lost another sub? Man, I think you're losing your touch," James replied, obviously teasing him, but deep down Alec admitted to himself that it pretty much described the situation. He had lost his last submissive to a Dom still wearing diapers, but according to Adele, the man had much more to offer her than he did. And so, he was alone again.

"Perhaps I should dedicate myself to meditation; I might be more successful in that field," he said, with yet another grimace.

"You have not been able to keep a submissive for longer than two or three months since Jasmine died in that car accident," his friend said, poking the wound.

Alec's face assumed his usual stoic look, and he pretended he hadn't heard his friend's conclusion. What nobody knew, was that the night Jasmine died, she was also leaving him. She had had enough of his lack of emotions and feelings, of his incapacity to make commitments and put his heart into the relationship.

Things were going bad, even back then.

"And where's Hannah? She didn't come with you tonight?" he asked instead, looking for the explosive redheaded brat that had become his friend's wife and submissive.

James' face lit up with a broad smile before he answered.

"She wasn't feeling very well tonight. You know they say: the first three months can be very difficult."

Alec looked at him puzzled for a second before he understood what the other man was saying.

"Hannah is pregnant?" he asked to confirm.

"Yes, six weeks now, can you believe it?" James answered showing all his pride and happiness.

"I see." And that was the only thing Alec managed to say. He didn't like Hannah. He thought she was nothing but a fraud, a gold digger who pretended to be a submissive just to hook his gullible friend.

"Aren't you going to congratulate me?" James asked, showing his hurt, in the face of his friend's non-reaction.

Alec sighed, and turned to face James.

"I guess that if it makes you happy, then I'm happy for you," he said, choosing his words carefully. After all James was his oldest friend.

"Man, I hate to see that Hannah is right about you. You've become a cold shell of the man that used to be my friend," James ranted, shaking his head in disbelief. "You're pushing everybody away from you. No wonder no one sticks around you anymore."

Alec thought about defending himself from James' accusations, but he simply was too tired.

He stood up and left the club, heading home. The night had been a total waste of time and as if that wasn't enough, he had lost one of his best friends.

Outside the club, he looked around for a taxi. It was a cold, damp night, with thick fog that perfectly matched his dark mood.

Impatient and unwilling to stay there any longer, he started walking down the street.

He must have walked for some ten to fifteen minutes when he heard footsteps getting closer. The person probably was a woman in heels judging by how the footsteps sounded, and she was running fast towards him.

He looked around, trying to see anything through the dense fog, hearing the footsteps getting closer and closer. All of a sudden, a small figure came out of nowhere and crashed against him, almost knocking him to the ground. His big, strong, muscled body absorbed the hit and was able to stop the human bullet. Her cry was muffled against his chest.

Katherine looked around. All of a sudden, the situation had gotten out of her control. The man she had been dancing with for the past few minutes looked at her with shameless hunger written all over his face. Although she had felt him getting closer and more reckless with every minute the dance continued, she thought he wouldn't dare to do much more than that. So, she decided to wait for the music to end and say goodbye politely.

Before she could do that, she felt another man getting closer from behind her, resting his hands over her hips. She looked over her shoulder to see the man who had been accompanying her dance partner throughout the entire night.

"Hey, what the fuck do you think you're doing?" she asked, getting his hands out of her. The man in front of her grabbed her hands together over his chest and the other one returned his hands to her hips, pressing his body tightly against hers, making her notice the bulge in his crotch.

"We just want to have some fun, the fun you've been promising us all night," he whispered in her ear and she could smell the liquor on his breath.

"I haven't been promising anything to anyone," she protested through clenched teeth, trying to free her hands from the first man's grip.

The man in front of her tightened his grip around her wrists and got even closer to her. They had her completely imprisoned between them and she was starting to feel desperate. How the hell had a simple dance turned into this?

Her instinct was to start yelling from the top of her lungs, but she was in a club where yells seemed to be normal, besides the music was so loud no one would hear her. She was starting to think she had made a very big mistake coming to a club like this alone. What had she been thinking?

Of nothing, actually, she had just acted on her instinct. Right, then she had to start using her brains and not her instinct. After all, her instinct always got her into trouble.

"Of course, you have. Your precious little body has been promising to take us to paradise ever since you came through that door, doll," the man in front of her said, sounding so lame she almost burst into laughter.

"Oh, that's so sweet, Hun, really sweet," she answered with her best impersonation of Dolly

Parton. "Why don't you boys let me go freshen up a little bit for you? I'll be back in a second."

"We'll walk you there, we would hate it if you got lost on your way." The one in front of her obviously wasn't as drunk as the other one and she would have more problems with him.

"Why, aren't you boys such gentlemen!" she said, without sincerity.

But they released her and walked her to the ladies' room.

Tonight wasn't her lucky night. Ladies' rooms in clubs were normally packed with women, but that night, at that moment, there was no one else there, no one she could ask for help.

She looked around looking for a way out and the only thing she could find was a small window that opened to the outside. She had her coat and purse stored in the club's reception area, but considering the alternative, she thought she could always come back some other day to pick them up.

"Come on, doll, we don't have all night," the man's call hastened the decision. She picked up a trash can, and standing on it, she threw herself out the window. For a short person like her, a fall from over six feet wasn't an easy thing and she whimpered out loud.

Still lying on the ground, she heard the men rush inside the bathroom and realize she had escaped.

The window was too small for either of them to get out through, and they soon realized it. That gave her an advantage she wanted to use, so she got up, ignoring her bruises and started running down the street, not knowing where the hell she was going, just trying to get away from them as fast as she could.

The fog was very thick and her heart thundered hard in her chest every time she saw a shadow moving.

She had left the club behind her a little while ago, when all of a sudden, she bumped in one of the shadows. She screamed at the top of her lungs, but her cry was muffled by the chest of the man holding her.

She struggled against him, scared as hell. The man was huge and obviously strong.

"Hey, watch it," he scolded the person that he realized was a woman.

She struggled in his arms to free herself.

"Let me go, you clumsy gorilla," she shouted, squirming harder.

He released her so suddenly that Katherine almost fell to the ground. Faster than expected for a man his size, he grabbed her again, helping her avoid falling.

He stabilized her, still grabbing her, waiting to hear a 'Thank you' from the little beast to no avail.

Katherine was grateful for not being on the ground again, but she was still scared of this person. And when she was scared she became foul-mouthed.

"Let me go, you idiot," she repeated, this time without shouting.

"Are you sure? Or will I need to grab you again?" he asked sarcastically.

"Just do it, damn I," she insisted again, holding back her desire to stamp her foot in sheer frustration. The man's touch was doing weird things to her senses and she didn't like it.

He finally released her again, and she stumbled a bit before she was able to stand firm on her own.

"Where were you going running like that in this weather?" he asked, in his best Dom tone, considering that the little brat certainly needed a few lessons in behavior, maybe some good old-fashioned spankings over her Dom's knee.

"That's none of your business. Because of you, I've lost precious seconds," she retorted, fixing her clothes.

As if to confirm her words, they both heard heavy footsteps running their way.

"Damn, damn," she mumbled enraged, as she started to run out of there.

"What's going on? Who's after you?" he asked, grabbing her by the arm, preventing her from fleeing the place.

"I don't have time for this, you stupid a…" she started saying through her teeth, the footsteps getting closer by the second.

He pulled her closer and covered her little dirty mouth with one of his big hands and she gasped, terrified. Silently, he dragged her out of the way, into a dark doorway, pressing her against it and covering her completely with his body. One of his hands was still over her mouth, preventing her from making any kind of sound, and the other one pinned her completely against the door.

Her hands clawed the hand covering her mouth and she tried to get it off her mouth, but he was so strong, and she wasn't even able to move it a tenth of an inch. His whole body was pressed against hers and she couldn't move at all.

The footsteps sounded closer, and they were able to tell they were running fast. Alone, she wouldn't have stood a chance against those two, but the darkness of the night and the fog worked in their favor and was more than enough to hide them from the two men chasing her, and they just ran right past them without noticing them.

Though she felt grateful for the man's help, she was furious, as well. He had treated her like a puppet he could move around at will.

Alec waited for a couple of minutes in the same position until he could no longer hear anything before he slowly released the woman.

The moment his hand loosened his grip over her mouth, the little beast showed her nature and she bit him, hard, deeply and painfully.

She was still furious by his rudeness, so she bit him until she felt the metallic taste of blood, not letting go until he was able to escape her teeth.

He managed to release his hand from her teeth, cursing. From his insides.

"You have a funny way of thanking those who help you," he said, oozing sarcasm.

"You deserve it. I don't remember asking for your help, you… you… gorilla!" she spurted as waves of mixed relief and anger rushed through her whole body.

"This should teach me not to help ungrateful strangers," he scolded himself shaking his hurt hand, wiping the blood she had ripped from him and turning around to walk away.

The night was even darker and the fog seemed thicker and he was having trouble leaving the little beast there alone, but there was no way of helping people who didn't want to be helped.

Katherine looked around, unable to see anything, scared of what might be hidden behind the shadows. She did not even have the money to grab a taxi home.

All her anger and rage disappeared being replaced by sheer fear.

He took a few steps away from her and to his relief her voice stopped him.

"Please… don't leave me here alone…" He stopped and she took a step towards him. "I'm sorry I bit you, I…"

He turned to look at her.

"Now you want the help of a… what was that you called me? Ah, yes, a clumsy gorilla?" he said, in a tone colder than the freezing breeze swirling around them, crossing his arms over his chest. She brushed her hands over her naked arms, starting to feel very cold.

"I'm sorry, ok? I was scared to death and you managed to scare me even more," she retorted, letting her bad temper take control.

Alec shook his head in disbelief and turned around again, done with her. The woman was truly ungrateful, and he had done more than enough helping her to hide from the guys chasing her. He could almost bet she had gotten herself into that situation through that big mouth of hers.

"God, what do you want from me, a written apology? I'll get you one as soon as I get home," she exploded, afraid he could actually leave her there. "I don't even know where I am, and I left my purse and my coat back at the club," she added in a plaintive tone.

He stopped, again shaking his head impatiently, before turning to look at her. Despite the dim light, he was able to see her naked arms and notice for the first time the absence of any warm piece of clothing.

"This is really my night," he whispered to himself, scolding all the gods of the universe.

He turned around and took off his coat and handed it to her, keeping his jacket.

She grabbed it reluctantly, putting it on. Her nostrils were invaded by a scent, a mix of sandalwood and musk that was enthralling. She took a deep breath and looked up at him.

"I had been walking for almost fifteen minutes and I didn't see any taxis, so I guess I better call one," he said, with resignation in his voice.

"Why haven't you called one from the start?" she asked, suspicious.

"Because I wanted to walk for a while, and good thing I did, don't you think? Otherwise, who knows what would have happened to you," he sneered..

He grabbed his cell phone and called the taxi company he usually used and asked to be picked up. They told him that due to the weather and the amount of people requiring their services it would take them at least an hour to get there.

Sighing with frustration, Alec made a decision and asked them to pick him up at his club.

"It will take them an hour to get here, so I've decided to wait for them back at the club where I was," he informed her.

"What if I don't want to go there with you?" she asked, furious with his authoritative tone. Who the hell did he think he was to order her around?

"Well, you can stay here, I'm sure your friends must be on their way back to the club, so you're free to stay here and wait for them," he answered in a very cold tone. He had lost all compassion he might have felt for the brat.

He started walking back to the club and she started following him only seconds later, muttering softly. He was determined to ignore anything else coming from her. When the taxi arrived at the club, he would get her into it, pay for it for her and send her home. Hopefully, he would have forgotten about her within ten seconds afterward.

She was having trouble walking in her heels. Her run for it had left blisters on her feet and it was hurting like hell, but she had no intention of letting him know that. So, she kept walking for a couple of minutes until the pain became unbearable.

She stopped for a few seconds and tried taking them off and walking barefoot, but the hard asphalt was almost frozen and was even worse.

She muttered, completely enraged with herself and the whole world. This was certainly a night to forget, forever.

She put on her shoes again, but she just couldn't take it anymore.

"Hey, you… mister," she called to him since he was a few steps ahead of her.

He didn't pay her any attention, so she tried again.

"Hey, come on, I know you heard me," she yelled at him, leaning against a lamppost.

He finally stopped and turned to look at her. They were almost at the club's entrance, so what could she possibly want?

"What's the matter now?" he asked, showing all his impatience.

"I can't take another step. Do you think you could send the taxi here when it arrives?" she explained briefly.

"We're a minute or two away from the club. I'm sure you can take that," he replied, furious at what looked like laziness on her part.

"Well, I can't. I'm not taking another single step," she insisted, crossing her arms over her chest.

He walked towards her, looking bigger than ever as he towered over her.

"Don't you think you have caused enough trouble, as it is, you little brat? I could be home by now, quietly enjoying my night, and instead of that, I'm out here in the cold, putting up with a spoiled little brat, who thinks her will is the most important thing in the world," he ranted, furious.

"Well, excuse me, sir, never mind me. Please go back to your quiet life, I won't bother you anymore," she answered, determined not to be intimidated by him.

He lost his temper. For the first time in a long time, he just lost it.

He grabbed her by her elbow and simply dragged her along behind him.

She gasped, surprised, the pain in her feet getting worse.

"Let me go! You have no right to do that!" she screeched, but he just ignored her. Tears started to run down her cheeks, the pain too hard to bear. "Let me go, please," she begged.

At first, he thought he wasn't hearing well. It looked as if she was crying, but that couldn't be right, could it?

He stopped and looked at her. They were under the dim light of a lamppost and he was able to see the tears running down her cheeks.

"Please, let me go," she repeated, freeing her arm from his grip.

"What's going on? Why are you crying?" he asked, cold, still suspicious.

"I can't walk anymore," she said again.

"Why not?" he asked, treating her like a stubborn little child.

"Because it hurts too much," she whispered, wiping the tears from her face.

"What?" he shouted astonished.

"My feet hurt too much, ok? High heels aren't designed for running, and I ran quite a bit," she finally explained.

He crouched and lifted her right foot, taking off her shoe. Her blisters were bleeding now and it was obvious she was in pain.

He rested her foot gently over her shoe and he got up.

"Why the hell didn't you tell me about it?" he asked angrily..

"I told you I couldn't walk anymore," she answered, reproachfully.

He looked at her, shaking his head in disbelief.

He picked up her shoes and gave them to her before he took her in his arms and carried her the rest of the way.

"You don't have to do this..." she started saying, feeling uncomfortable.

"Please, do me a favor, will you? Be quiet for a couple of minutes," he asked, still enraged over her behavior.

She snorted but didn't say anything else.

Chapter Three

It only took him a couple of minutes to get to the club. He rang the bell and waited for the security guard to open the door.

"Sir Alec, I didn't think you would be back," the man said, surprised to see him carrying a woman.

"Neither did I, John," Alec answered, entering the room and standing her up on the soft carpet. "Please tell Mike I'm here with a guest. I'll take her to one of the private rooms," he asked, politely, "A taxi will come to pick us up, so I'd appreciate it if you'd let me know when it arrives,"

"Sure thing, Sir. What room will you use?"

"Is the blue room empty?" Alec asked.

"Yes, Sir, it is."

"Good. I'll use it then.

Katherine was so astonished with the place that she didn't react immediately.

"Wait! What? I'm not going anywhere with you," she protested.

Having lost his last thread of patience, Alec simply carried her again and took her to the blue room ignoring her protests.

He opened the room, took her to the bed, and unceremoniously dropped her onto it.

Katherine let out a small cry and tried to get up.

"I swear to god that if you get up from that bed, I'll tie you to it and gag you as well," he threatened her, his tone as cold as ice.

"You can't do that," she protested, but she didn't make a move.

"Don't try me," he warned her.

He approached her and helped her out of his coat.

For the first time, he was able to see her clearly. She was petite. She couldn't be taller than five feet, thin, but with generous curves, long blonde hair and a face that made you think of naughty elves.

She was wearing a sleeveless, short, black dress and her legs were covered with black stockings, completely ruined by her attempt to walk without her shoes. He went to the bathroom to pick up a first aid box, returning to the room to treat the blisters.

"There's no need for you to do that. I can take care of that when I get home," she said, feeling uncomfortable. She was sitting on the edge of the bed, her legs hanging from it.

He knelt in front of her and put both of her feet on his hard thighs.

"I'll be the judge of that," he said, coldly and she decided to let him do it. It was useless discussing things with him. His will was harder than titanium.

He rolled down her ruined stockings, and every time he touched her, every time his fingers brushed her skin, she felt rushes of energy running wildly through her body. Carefully, he cleaned the wounds and neatly covered them with gauze pads. His touch wasn't doing much to help her keep her self-control. She could hear the thundering of her heart against her chest.

Trying to think of something else other than his touch, she took the opportunity to look at him carefully. Even on his knees he looked tall. He was way over six feet, with a broad, strong, muscular body. And as if that wasn't enough, the man looked way too handsome. It was a pity he was nothing more than a presumptuous, cold, arrogant troll.

"There you go. That's the best I can do." He finished cleaning her other foot and took the first aid box back to the bathroom.

"Thank you. I'm sorry I caused you so much trouble," she said when he returned. She looked around the room, feeling a bit uncomfortable. After all, she was in a bedroom with a total stranger, sitting on a huge bed.

As her gaze took in more detail, she gasped, surprised. The bedroom was no ordinary room. Hanging from the ceiling were a few chains, the bed had cuffs attached to both the headboard and footboard and in a corner, there was a spanking bench.

"What kind of club is this?" she asked, in a murmur.

"It's just a club. Don't worry about that," he retorted, cold as ice.

She was starting to think the man was colder than Jack Frost. He sure was able to throw droplets of ice your way like sharp daggers.

"Please, answer me," she asked, her curiosity reaching the highest levels.

"It's just a club, a private one," he repeated, not willing to give her any details.

"It's a BDSM club, isn't it?" she insisted.

He ignored her question taking a seat in an armchair used for spankings. He was tired. The night had been a real nightmare and he was desperate to put the woman in a taxi and forget he had ever met her.

She jumped out of bed, burying her feet on the thick carpet as she walked towards the spanking bench. She had never seen one, other than in pictures, and she ran her hands over it, checking the cuffs, the red leather upholstery, and the smoothness of the wood.

"What is this for?" she asked, her curiosity stronger than her common sense. "Are you a Dom, a submissive or…?" she asked again, teasing him, without looking at him, still examining the bench.

He didn't answer, and she turned to look at him.

His face was a perfect mask, made of the hardest rock and she felt a shiver ran down her spine.

Alec looked at the woman running her fingers over the spanking bench, with an unconscious caress. Her curiosity bothered him, and he had no intention whatsoever of satisfying it.

He had brought her to this room because it was one of the simplest in the club, and because he couldn't leave her in the reception area, seeing everyone who came and went from the place.

They had very good reasons to keep the club private and exclusive for members only.

"God, are you sure you're made of flesh and blood?" she spurted, upset with his refusal to answer her simple question, hating the impassivity of his expression.

He got up and took a few steps towards her.

She stepped back. One thing was for sure: the man was dangerous.

"Do you want me to prove it to you?" he asked, with a low, hoarse tone of voice that ripped shudders from her body.

"No, thank you, you don't have to prove anything to me," she answered, taking another step back. "Can you call the taxi company and see if they are close to getting here?" she asked, changing the subject and walking discreetly towards the door. He stretched out one arm and grabbed her by her wrist pulling her closer to him.

"Maybe I feel the need to prove it to you," he said, looking her straight in the eyes.

"No… I'm sure you… don't feel that," she stammered, feeling rushes of energy flowing through her whole body, from where his hand touched her skin, her heart thundering in her chest.

He grabbed her other wrist and pulled her even closer, as he leaned his head towards hers.

"You have no idea what I feel and what I don't," he said and his words sounded so threatening, she shuddered even more.

He released her wrists and cupped her face with both hands, claiming a hard, deep kiss from her lips, his tongue penetrating her mouth, assailing every single corner of it, making it his, completely and indisputably his.

His hands pulled her even closer and she was able to feel the warmness of his body radiating heat to hers. She threw her hands around his waist, completely lost in the swirl of emotions his touch and his lips awakened in her.

He finally let her breathe. One of his hands grasped her mane, pulling her head back, exposing her sensitive skin to him, as his mouth drew a trail of fire with kisses and nibbles along her cheeks to her ears, down her neck, across her shoulder line and back up to her mouth again, setting a wildfire within her, making her moan out loud.

His other hand ran down from her face to one of her breasts and he cupped it, barely fitting it in his palm, his fingers burying themselves in her tender skin with a tight squeeze, ripping shudders of pure desire from her body.

In that moment, someone knocked on the door, and he slowly removed his lips from hers, giving them one last nibble before he raised his head.

"The taxi is here, Sir Alec," the security guard's voice sounded on the other side of the door..

"Thank you, John," he answered, his eyes still locked on hers, his breath as heavy as hers. "It seems you were saved by the bell, little brat," he said, letting her go. "A piece of advice; be careful when you play with fire. You might get seriously burned."

She gulped but decided to remain silent.

He handed her his coat, trying to help her put it back on.

"Maybe I shouldn't wear your coat," she said.

"It's cold outside. You can return it later," he said, his tone not allowing any refusal from her.

He helped her walk to the taxi, and to her surprise, he didn't get in with her. He paid the taxi driver and told him to drive her to wherever she wanted to go, and said goodbye.

"Take care. I can't say it was a pleasure knowing you, but it sure was interesting," he said when she was already inside the taxi.

She snorted and said nothing else.

Her mind struggled between two opposite feelings: relief and disappointment. Knowing she would never see him again didn't feel right. Actually, it felt more wrong than anything she had ever felt in her life. But she had no intention of doing anything to fix that.

He obviously was out of her league and she would be better off without him in her life.

"Thank you for your help," she said, in a cold tone without even looking at him. He closed the door and the taxi left.

Alec stayed there watching the car disappear into the dark night and sighed, not sure whether he was relieved of disappointed. The little brat seemed to be something special.

Chapter Four

Katherine woke up the next morning and her first conscious thought was of him. Somehow, she knew she would have a hard time forgetting him and the way he had affected her. Especially when she knew he was a Dom, a real one, and not one of the fakes she kept meeting at the BDSM clubs she was able to visit, like the ones she had met the night before, She should know by now that going alone to a place like that wasn't the smartest thing to do, but her best friend Lucy had cancelled at the last minute, and she just didn't want to stay home.

Despite all of the night's distress, she was happy she had gone to the club. If she hadn't, she wouldn't have met him, and even if she never saw him again, he had made her believe again that finding a real Dom wasn't just a dream.

She got up reluctantly, her feet still extremely sore. It was a good thing it was Saturday and she didn't have to go to work until Monday.

Anyway, she would have to go back to the BDSM club to get her coat and her purse with her cell phone in it, but she intended to go during the afternoon since she didn't want to take the risk of meeting last night's trolls. She would also have to return his coat. The thing was made of expensive cashmere and it probably cost more than she made in a month.

The phone rang and she realized that must have been what woke her up. She grabbed it from her nightstand.

"Hello?"

"Katherine, don't tell me you went alone to the club last night." Lucy's voice almost left her deaf. "I called you like a hundred times last night."

Katherine frowned and prepared herself for her friend's scolding.

"Ok, I'm not telling you that."

"Oh, I knew it. You can be so stubborn. Do you know just how dangerous that could have been?"

"Actually, yes, I have a pretty good idea," she answered with a self-deprecating grin.

"*What happened*?" Lucy's shout almost pierced her tympanum.

"Nothing serious, I swear, just met the usual trolls, that's all," she answered, not lying, just bending the truth a little.

"*It's useless trying to make you be more sensible, right*?" Lucy scolded her, and Katherine could imagine her friend shaking her head in despair.

"What can I say? You know me better than anyone," she admitted. "How are you feeling today?" Lucy hadn't gone with her because she had had a terrible headache.

"I'm feeling just great. So do you want to go out tonight? We could go to that same club."

"I don't think I should be going there for a while. Besides, I still feel a bit tired." Katherine explained looking at her sore feet. She was still wearing the gauze bandages Sir Alec had put on them.

"Well, maybe it's better then. I'm going out with the other girls. Let me know if you change your mind," Lucy offered.

"Thank you, I will. Have a great time."

She spent the rest of the morning trying to clean her place without making her feet even sorer. Around five o'clock in the afternoon she took a taxi and went back to the club area. She wanted to go first to his club and drop off his coat, to diminish the probabilities of running into him. She would have to figure out which of the several clubs around was the one he had taken her to.

When she reached the last street, she decided to ask the driver if he knew of a private club around those parts. Luckily, he did, and when he left her in front of a huge wooden door, she knew she was in the right place. She paid the driver and hopped out of the taxi.

Feeling a bit nervous, she walked towards the door and rang the bell. She knew he wouldn't be around, but even so, she couldn't help feeling a bit nervous.

The same security guard opened the door.

"Hi there, remember me? I came in last night with Sir Alec," she said, with a hesitant smile.

"Ah, yes, the lady he brought in, carried in his arms," the man answered with an amused smile.

"Yes, that was me," she answered, unable to stop the blush covering her cheeks.

"How are you feeling today, Miss? I'm John, by the way, the security guard, at your service."

"I'm fine, thank you. It's a pleasure meeting you officially, John," she answered with a friendly grin. "You see, John, he lent me his coat last night, and I wanted to return it to him. Do you think I could leave it here for him?" she asked, showing him the piece of clothing folded over her arm.

"I think you can do even better," the man answered, surprising her. "Why don't you give it back to him yourself?" he asked.

Startled, she took a step back, shaking her head.

"No, there's no need for that. I would hate to bother him for such an insignificant thing," she answered, stretching the coat out to him.

"Oh, but I'm sure he would be bothered if you didn't return it personally," the man insisted, picking up the internal phone and calling someone.

"Sue, dear, can you please tell Sir Alec someone is here at the door asking for him? Thank you, love." He said to whoever answered the phone on the other end.

"No… really, there is no need to bother him. I'm sure he must be very busy. I'll just leave the coat here and go home," she said trying to hand the damn coat to the man. She didn't want to see the man again, she wasn't that crazy.

But the guard ignored her efforts and didn't take the coat.

A few minutes later, the door behind the guard opened, and he came out.

Chapter Five

She felt her breath getting caught in her lungs when she saw him. With black leather pants and a t-shirt that enhanced every single one of his muscles, he looked simply devastating. She took a deep breath and tried to get a hold of herself.

"Ah, here he is," the guard said, turning to look at him. "This young lady came by to return your coat, Sir Alec."

"I was just trying to leave it here at the reception," Katherine explained, frowning at his cold expression. The man was a real ice floe. She was sure if she could remember his expression while he was kissing her the night before, he would have had the same remote expression on his face. Nothing seemed to affect him. "I told him there was no need to bother you."

Alec looked at the little beast, and the appellative no longer sounded right. Her long, golden mane fell down her back, in soft threads of silk, and her white skin looked bright and smooth, and though she still had that look of a naughty elf, it sure was a beautiful one. He looked at John wishing he could strangle him for making him face this woman again, after spending the whole night with her on his mind.

"It's alright, but you didn't have to bother bringing the coat. I have others," he said in the coldest tone he was able to produce.

"I'm sure you do, but I don't like to keep things that don't belong to me," she said, feeling the rage starting to boil inside her. "Here, take it," she handed him the coat and he grabbed it as someone would grab something infectious. "Now that you have it, you can burn it if you want. Have a good day," she added turning around and heading towards the door. 'Damn man.'

She never made it to the door. He threw the coat to the amused John and with two strides, he was next to her, grabbing her arm and stopping her from leaving.

"There's no need to be rude," he said.

"I'm the one being rude? Well, now, you sure have a funny perspective of reality," she said, shaking his hand off her arm. "Now, if you don't mind, I have another club to visit."

Alec looked at her puzzled for just a second until he figured she had to be talking about the club she had run away from the night before.

"Are you going back to the other club?" he asked, and his severe tone told her exactly what he thought about the idea.

"Yes, of course. I left my coat and my purse there, remember? Besides, that's none of your business." She answered, trying to mimic his coldness.

"Do you think that's a good idea? What if the guys are still around?" he asked, obviously mad at her.

"I doubt they even remember my face. I have to go now; your chit chat is delaying me," she pointed out and opened the door.

Alec went back to where John was avidly watching the whole scene, still holding Alec's coat in his arms. Alec grabbed it, rudely, putting it on and stomped out of the club behind the stubborn woman, yelling back at John:

"I won't be long."

When he reached the street, she was a few steps away, waiting for a taxi.

"If you insist in going back there, I will take you," he announced as soon as he reached her.

"Please don't bother. This is none of your business," she insisted without even looking at him.

"Well, I'm making it my business. Come, I have my car just around the corner," he demanded, taking her by an elbow.

Katherine tried to release herself from his grip, and though the grip wasn't tight, it was impossible for her to free herself.

She sighed, defeated.

"If I let you go with me, will you promise I'll never have to see your bitter face again in my life?" she asked, furious.

"Believe me, I'll do all in my power to see to it," he answered with a grimace.

"Good!" she replied, letting him drag her to his car, a black European car that looked very expensive. He asked her for the club's address and in less than five minutes he was parking his car in front of the BDSM club. She hopped out of the car and headed to the place's door. A security guard let them in as soon as she explained the purpose of their visit.

Alec, behind her, looked at the place with a horrified expression. The place looked really cheap and was decorated as a very low budget dungeon. The BDSM devices looked like props and not something you could actually use. What in hell had she been doing there in the first place?

The guard retrieved her coat and purse, and they were able to leave the dreadful place.

He helped her in the car and took his seat behind the wheel, but he didn't start the car. He sat there looking ahead.

Katherine cleared her throat loudly, looking at him.

"Is there a problem? Now that you have done your daily good deed, I can grab a taxi home from here," she said, getting a bit nervous from his expression.

"What were you looking for in a place like that? Do you know what kind of club that is?" he asked in a very upset tone.

"I fail to see what any of that has to do with you. I'm over eighteen you know, and I don't need another father figure in my life, believe me, so drop it," she ranted, not willing to accept more scolding from the man.

"That's a lousy sex club, where people go to get laid, under the poor excuse they're into BDSM!" he almost shouted.

"So what? It's my life! I can do with it whatever I feel like doing," she shouted back. "Do you know what? Thank you for your help," she added and put her hand on the door handle to open the door.

In that precise moment, a click was heard inside the car, as he pressed a button, and all the doors locked.

"Not yet, I'm not done with you," he told her, looking at her.

"What's the matter with you?" she asked, furious. "Why do you care? You're just a stranger, damn it."

He looked at her with no expression on his face.

"Let's say I feel responsible for the life I saved last night," he said, but it was obvious he didn't feel it at all.

Katherine crossed her arms over her chest, frustrated. She sighed and decided that the fastest way to get rid of him was to satisfy his curiosity.

"What do you want know?" she said, looking straight ahead through the car's windshield.

"Why did you come to this club?"

The man went straight to the jugular, right to the killing zone.

"Well, it's a BDSM club, what do you think I was looking for?" she answered, sarcastically.

"Don't beat around the bush," he warned her.

"Very well, my last boyfriend was into BDSM, he used to tie me in bed, and play rough, and I had to admit it excited me a lot, so I read a couple of books and saw some movies about it and I felt I should investigate this BDSM thing a bit more. And I have been doing so, for the past year. I've been to several munches, I've met a lot of people that actually live in the lifestyle, and I've been looking around," she admitted to him, more than she had ever done to anyone else. Even Lucy thought she was just curious.

"What happened to your boyfriend?" he asked.

"Well, he told me he was a switch, but he met a woman that convinced him that being her submissive was his goal in life, so we went different directions," she explained. There hadn't been any broken hearts there. She'd had a lot of fun with him, but her heart had never been involved, not deeply anyway.

"And on what side of the slash do you think you are?" he asked in a very derogatory tone.

"Really? Why the hell should I answer that? You're already judging me without knowing me or knowing my interests," she answered, sarcastically, "I have nothing more to say to you, so you either open the door for me or drive me back to your club."

Alec looked at her, sitting next to him, her little body stiffened, her eyes locked on some invisible point. The truth was he couldn't explain to himself why he wanted to know everything about her. He turned the car on and drove back to the club with a decided expression on his face. So she wanted to experience BDSM? He was going to give her the experience of her life.

He arrived at the club, parked in his usual place, and helped her out of the car.

"Thank you for your help," she said, as soon as she stepped on   the sidewalk.

"I have a proposal for you," he said, betting on her curious, almost reckless side. "I'm sure you'll find it very alluring."

Katherine looked at him, astonished. The man was a big box of surprises. Every time she thought she had seen everything, he came out with something else. A proposal? What could he possibly have to propose to her?

Chapter Six

"Let's hear it." Her curiosity wouldn't allow anything else.

Alec almost sighed with relief. He had her.

"You said you have been investigating the lifestyle, right?" he asked, looking her, straight in the face, attentive to any expression, any subtle change that would let him know what way to proceed.

"Yes, I believe we've established that," she said impatiently.

"This club is one of the best BDSM clubs in the country. Here you won't find fake Dom's or fake submissives," he said, making a larger pause between sentences, which allowed him to see the sudden shine in her eyes when he mentioned Dom's. If you added that to the way she had reacted last night to his touch, he was quite sure she was a submissive, even with the enormous brat attitude she had. She longed for a Dom in her life, and he intended to give her one--him.

"So? I don't think all the Dom's and subs I've met are fakes," she replied, suspiciously.

"Of course not, but here you'll see the real thing. Remember how much you liked that spanking bench you saw last night in the bedroom?" he asked, playing carefully with his cards. Sometimes he felt he was dealing with a time bomb. Any false move and everything simply blew up.

"Yes, I remember," she conceded.

"Well, we have all kinds of devices inside. And who knows, you might get the chance of using them as you best see fit. I would take you under my protective wing and show you everything."

"Let's say I agree to this. What exactly would that imply?" she asked, still not convinced.

"I would become your tutor, I would show you around, and show you whatever you might want to try. I'm a hard player, but I'm sure you would be just fine with it."

"I can get out any minute I want?" she asked, feeling more compelled to accept than she thought possible.

"Just say your safe word and you'll be out." And that did it, he could tell, so he lost no time. Holding her by her elbow, he gently led her back to the club's entrance. He invited her in and took her to a small table in a corner.

"You need to fill out a few forms before you're authorized to enter as my guest," he explained, handing her a few sheets. "One is a Non-Disclosure Agreement everybody has to sign in order to get in."

"Very well." She grabbed the papers and started to read. Like he said, one was a basic NDA and she signed it with no problem. The other sheets, on the other hand, were a complete inquiry into a person's kinks, limits, and experience. No wonder he hadn't insisted on asking more. She filled it in the best she could, fighting the desire to complete some of the questions with something scandalous. After all, it could actually be the guy's favorite kink. She wasn't that insane... well, most of the time. She was there, wasn't she? With him, the man she had no intention of seeing, ever again.

Alec looked at her filling out the forms. Those inquiries were the best thing they had implemented. It gave them a pretty good idea of what their members and guests might be looking for, and when it came to a new submissive, it would tell the Dom just how far they could go, which limits he could push and which he should never consider.

The woman finally finished the forms, signed them and handed them to Alec. He checked her signature and a grimace of acceptance curved his lips.

"Katherine… how appropriate," he said.

"And what's that supposed to mean?" she asked, getting up, resting her hands on her hips, in a defiant position.

"You've reminded me of the main character of *The Taming of the Shrew*, Katherine, ever since I saw you for the first time," he explained, answering her defiance.

"No kidding? And I still wonder why I find you so obnoxious," she mumbled, loud enough for him to hear her.

He chuckled and continued reading her forms. She didn't have much experience, other than the one she had with guy she had already mentioned. She had tried some bondage workshops, directed by known riggers, but that was basically all she had tried.

He looked her over, head to toe, and noticed the gauze on her feet.

"How are your blisters?" he asked.

"Much better, thank you," she answered, blushing a bit, remembering what happened just after that.

"Good, I guess you're ready to get in. We'll start by taking a walk around the place for you to take a look and decide if you want to try anything," he said, taking her by her elbow and leading her to a coat room. "Leave your coat and purse here. Make sure you leave the club with them," he advised, unable to make his tongue refrain.

She showed her tongue to his back, but in that precise moment he turned to look at her and caught a glimpse of it. He closed his expression even more, and she was sure, right then and there, he was dying to lay his hands on her, preferably on her tender buttocks.

She giggled and followed him out of the coat room after leaving her belongings there.

Her first step into the club's main room was quite similar to entering another dimension. The place was nothing like any of the clubs she had ever been in before. The décor was sober, elegant and luxurious with couches of burgundy velvet, small round tables of dark wood, a bar in a corner and a big stage in the middle. Here and there, you could see small areas for those more exhibitionist, with all kinds of benches, and even a couple of Saint Andrew's cross.

"The good stuff is downstairs in the dungeons, and we also have several semi-private dungeons and private rooms as well, like the one I took you to last night," he informed her, whispering in her ear, to make himself heard over the music and the people talking. His breath on her ear was enough to send shudders down her spine, and she had to make a huge effort to control her body and not let him know just how much he affected her.

"Can you take me there?" she asked him, and he nodded, resting his big hand on the middle of her back, guiding her in the right direction. She was able to feel the heat from his hand going through the thin fabric of her top. She couldn't quite understand why a simple brush from him was enough to set her on fire.

He took her downstairs and there they found a lot of people engaged in all kinds of play.

"Isn't it a bit early for this number of people?" she asked, curious. It still wasn't seven o'clock at night and the place was crowded.

"We're celebrating a special weekend. That's why there are so many people around here, at this hour." He walked her through the place, stopping for a few minutes when she wanted to watch a particular scene.

So far, Alec had noticed her huge interest in ropes, all kinds of ropes. She had appreciated a simple corset made of silky ropes, but she had watched even more carefully how one of the riggers was placing a submissive in a *strappado.* The scene had been quite hot and he was able to see how much she would have loved to be in the other woman's place. He knew her level of arousal were spiraling up, and that was more and more obvious by the hard tips of her big, round breasts.

"Alec, my friend, it's good to see you down here," a man's voice behind them distracted the couple watching a sensuous flogging on a cross.

Alec turned around and looked over his shoulder.

"Jonas, how are you?" he greeted, in his usual tone, distant and cold.

"A new sub? I don't believe I've seen her face around here before," the man asked, looking intensely at Katherine.

She had turned to see who he was talking to, sadly surprised to see the man was an iceberg with everybody. But she almost wished she hadn't. The man, Alec had called Jonas, was one of those men she always tried to stay away from. Something in him gave her goosebumps in a very unpleasant way.

Unconsciously, she moved closer to Alec, out of the man's possible reach.

"Yes, she is mine." Alec's sentence was simple and yet incredibly clear. And though she could have discussed that 'mine', she certainly would never do it in front of this guy. She would settle things with Sir Alec later.

"You always manage to get the most beautiful ones. But you never seem to keep them long, so there's still hope," the man said before he walked away.

"In your dreams!" she said, loud enough for Alec to hear her. "That's a very repulsive man," she said, lowering her tone.

"You think so? He seems to have a lot of success with the ladies," he said.

"Well that won't ever happen with me," she replied, shuddering with disgust. "About that mi..." she started to say, ready to scold him for saying she was his, but she never managed to finish her sentence.

Chapter Seven

He leaned down, cupping her face with his hands, claiming a fierce, deep kiss from her lips, ripping any coherent thought from her mind, just leaving feelings and sensations.

His fingers explored her face, her ears, her neck, while his mouth assailed every corner of hers, stealing her breath, turning her into a shuddering doll.

His hands ran down her back, pulling her even closer to him, for a few more moments until his hunger became too wild.

He stopped, immediately. There were many more things he wanted to do that night and sex might or might not be a part of them. He took a step back enjoying the fuzzy expression on the little shrew's face.

"Have you decided what you would like to try?" he asked, taking dissimulated deep breaths.

"I believe it would be best for me to go home," she said, more thinking to herself, than really talking to him.

"I don't believe that you're getting cold feet so soon," he teased her, shamelessly poking her to get her to stay. "Don't you want to try some ropes or even the sweet kiss of a flogger on your skin?"

"I don't think it's a good idea to be doing that with a stranger," she answered, trying to sound as cold as he always did. She was still fighting off the devastating effects of that damn kiss, so she wasn't up to putting herself even more in his hands.

Feeling her nervousness, Alec decided to play foul. He wanted to have her, and he was determined to get what he wanted.

With the tip of his finger, he traced a road from her neck, down and around her breasts, simulating the trail a rope would take.

"We're not strangers anymore, don't you think? Just imagine, ropes around your neck, down to your chest, circling your breasts tightly, making them tense up, like you've never felt them before, then catching your arms behind your back, pulling them up, leaving you helpless and exposed to the one on the other end of the rope."

The image he was creating with his words, added to the brushing of his finger, had her breathless again. Her chest heaved beneath his touch and she could feel her arousal peaking to unexpected levels.

"You want to do it," he said, and for once, his tone wasn't cold or scoffing. He was alluring, exciting, exuding the rawest passion she had ever experienced. "Give yourself to me for tonight, just this night, and I'll take you to places you didn't know existed. Just say yes to me," he added, stretching his hand toward her, his palm up, inviting hers to join his.

She fell completely under his spell, and her lips whispered what he wanted to hear.

"Yes."

He smiled, pleased, not victorious, and that finished her off. She surrendered to him, her hand lying meekly in his.

Alec cleared his throat, shaking the incomprehensible feelings her surrender had evoked in him. This was just two people having a good time, with nothing more than pleasure being exchanged.

He decided to take her to a private room. He doubted she was ready to show her naked body in public, and somehow he preferred that too, that night. He didn't feel like sharing, not even the delicious sight of her.

He chose one of the rooms he knew had a good cross and a spanking bench, and all the tying and suspension options all the rooms had. That would give him enough to work with. He wanted her to live all of the experiences possible of being tied for the first time. So, he intended to go easy on her and go slowly, very slowly, even if impatience already burned worse than hell deep inside him.

He wanted to make tonight for her, at least most of it. After all, he was no saint or monk.

Katherine followed Alec through several halls and stairs, but they were stopped again, this time, by a couple. The man was around Alec's age, mid-thirties, and the woman was probably around her age. She was an amazing redhead, with the greenest eyes she had ever seen, and the man could be Alec's brother. They had the same build and the same coloration.

"Alec, how are you?" the man greeted, and Katherine was able to sense some tension between them.

Alec looked at James and Hannah and considered grabbing the olive branch James was handing him, but then he looked at Hannah and decided it was pointless. He wasn't going to change his mind about her, and that would always come between him and James. So it was better to just finish it, right there and then.

"James, Hannah," he said, his tone cold, and it was obvious he was displeased with this encounter.

"Won't you introduce us to your friend?" James asked. The man was trying to cross the walls Alec had around him but to no avail.

"I don't think so," his cold answer made everyone else gasp in surprise.

"What's the matter with you? Why are you acting like an arrogant bastard?" James asked, his eyes showing just how much he was hurt.

Alec didn't answer; he simply remained in silence, waiting for them to leave.

"Because he is one, James. Let's go," Hannah said and managed to take James out of there.

Katherine looked at Alec. His face was a stone-carved mask, and she was starting to doubt her decision to get involved with this man.

"Let's go," he said, clearly with no intention of talking about the recent event. He led her again, as if nothing had happened, down the corridor, but then he stopped.

Alec rubbed his face with his hand, realizing he wasn't in the mood for this any longer. He turned to her. "I'm afraid I just remembered I have an appointment tonight I had forgotten. Can we reschedule this? For next Saturday at 07:00 pm?"

Katherine looked at him trying to figure what had changed, but his expression didn't reveal anything.

"Yes, of course, there's no problem," she nodded, accepting the possibility he had lost interest in her.

"So, can I expect you next Saturday? I'll let you a special pass at the entrance," he asked.

'Or maybe not,' she thought. "Yes, I'll be here."

"Good, see you then," he said, escorting her quickly to the main room. "You can stay for a while longer if you want. Have fun." Those were his last words before leaving her in the middle of the room, and walking away.

Katherine looked around a bit overwhelmed and decided she would better off to go back home.

Chapter Eight

Alec decided to go home immediately. He was in no mood to stick around another minute at the club. There, the silent house greeted him, making his dreariness feel even stronger, so he headed to his private gym. Practicing with his whip always relaxed him and tonight he needed it--a lot.

He took off his shoes, socks and shirt and prepared a big, white sheet of paper that he usually used in his practices and grabbed his favorite bullwhip.

After the first few strikes, he started to feel better, but he continued until there was not a piece of the paper hanging and his body was covered in sweat.

He put the whip away and headed to the shower in the bathroom inside the dungeon, dropping his pants and underwear on his way. Though he was feeling better, he still felt restless, angry.

He dreaded the fact that Hannah had managed to come between him and James, a man he considered more than family, a man that had been his unconditional friend ever since they met in high school.

He took a long, cold shower, letting the icy droplets hit his body until he felt numb. He dried himself and with no desire to go to his bedroom he jumped in the dungeon's bed and closed his eyes, trying to shut the world out.

'Alec woke up startled and sat on the bed. Someone had called his name.

"Alec, son," he turned his face and he saw his father standing next to the bed, as a blurry vision.

"Dad?" his tone revealed his confusion and his disbelief. His father had been dead for ten years now.

"Yes, Alec," the spectrum confirmed, "Son, what are you doing with your life? You're pushing everybody away from you, can't you see that?"

"I'm not pushing anyone away. They leave of their own free will," he protested, rubbing his eyes, sure he was having a weird dream, but feeling it was too damn real.

"You don't let them in your heart, and that's why they leave," his father assured, looking at him with regret, "Am I the one responsible for this? For the way you are?"

"Of course not. If someone's responsible, it's not you."

"Oh, but I believe I am. I always blamed your mother for leaving me, for not trying to keep our family together, but that wasn't true."

"How can you say that? She was the one who left," Alec protested.

"But I was the one absent. Don't you remember how many times I failed you? How many times I was supposed to be there for you, and I wasn't?"

"I don't remember any of that."

"But you must. Deep within, you're a good man, Alec, much better than me. You just need to remember how to love, how to believe in people and let them come closer to you," his father begged him.

Alec shook his head in denial, "You're looking at me through the eyes of a father."

"Son, just open your mind and your heart, and you'll see things clearer. You'll be visited by three spirits: the Spirit of the Past, the Spirit of the Present and the Spirit of the Future. Receive them willingly and learn from what they'll show you," his father warned him.

"You have to be kidding me, Dad!" he snorted.

"Remember, open your heart and mind, Son," his father said before he vanished into thin air.

Starting to think he was losing his mind, Alec lay back in bed, and closed his eyes for a second.

The sound of a whip cracking in the air made him open his eyes immediately, and sit up in bed again.

At the footboard of the bed, stood a huge old man, dressed in black leather, with gray hair, and holding a bullwhip in his hand. His face was marked with the signs of a well-lived life, his blue eyes sparkled with so much life that it hurt to look at them.

"You have to be kidding me!" Alec said with a dry laugh.

The man cracked the whip, this time hitting him hard on his thigh with it. "Did that felt as if I'm kidding, newbie?"

The man's hoarse voice reminded him of the first Dom he had ever met, when he was eighteen and exploring the trails that were leading him into BDSM. He used to call him newbie, too.

"No." And it didn't. He could feel the sting of the strike in his thigh and he looked at the man, intrigued.

"Who are you?"

"I thought they had sent your father to explain things to you," he ranted.

"So you're one of the so-called Spirits?" Alec shook his head. It was definite; he had lost his mind.

"Be more respectful newbie. I'm the Spirit of the Past, and I'm here to take you to your past."

"Oh, come on!"

The man walked around the bed and pulled him roughly by his elbow. "Let's go, I don't have all night."

Alec felt as if his body was being dragged through a vortex, and all of a sudden, he was floating over a football field. He recognized the scene; it had been one of the most important football games he had when he was ten. He was playing on the field, but his attention was on the public, looking for his father, but he still wasn't there.

"Do you remember that game?" the old man asked him.

"Yes, I do," he answered in a low voice.

"He never showed up. Your mother was there for you, always, but you wanted your father to see you winning that game."

Alec saw his friends carrying him after the winning point. His mother was standing there, and when his friends let him down, he ran to her open arms.

He could even hear her. "I'm sorry sweetheart." After that, she took him for pizza and ice cream with his best friend at the time.

"How many times did your father pull that one on you? How many times did he pull that one on your mother?" the old man asked, and Alec had to admit it had been too many. Her mother had started to lose her joy, her smile was a rare thing when she finally gave up and admitted her defeat; his father wasn't going to change.

The old man dragged him to another scene, one he would rather not see again, that was engraved by fire in his mind--the day his mother had left. He was 16 years old.

His mother was in the living room with his father arguing once more, and he was hiding behind the kitchen door.

"I can't stand this anymore. I'm supposed to be married to you and I feel worse than a widow. You're never there for me, we no longer live as a couple," his mother was complaining.

"I'm working to provide you with all the fancy things you obviously appreciate," he retorted.

"I would much rather feel that I still have a husband, John…"

"I'm giving you all that I can," he replied in a very cold tone.

"Well, it's not enough, it never has been, but I just can't take it anymore." He could hear the defeat in her mother's voice and see the tears running down her cheeks.

"Well you're free to go find more elsewhere." The cold words of his father made his mother gasp in pain, and with a final look at her husband, she left the room. The next morning she had left the house forever. She had tried to make Alec understand her reasons, but he had given his back on her. He had refused to see or talk to her ever since, despite the number of times she had tried. After a few years she had stopped trying and he supposedly felt relieved, but it seemed to reinforce his idea she really didn't love him. For him, she hadn't loved him enough to stay with him.

He could see now, he had acted like a hurtful, selfish teenager.

"Your mother still thinks of you. She stopped trying to talk to you, but she seeks for any little news she can get on you and she goes to your office once in a while and waits to see you leave." The old man's voice felt like a stab to his heart. That couldn't be true. He was sure she had forgotten she had a son a long time ago. The same way he had forgotten he had a mother.

Once more, the old man dragged him to another scene--the day he met James. James was the new kid at school and his size and strength made the school's bullies see him as a threat to their kingdom of terror.

Alec was a loner, having the same built as James, people feared to go near him.

That day, the bullies had cornered James. It was an unfair match, 6 to 1, and for a moment, Alec had considered ignoring the scene and just going home, j but he couldn't. He joined James, and although they didn't win that fight, it made them inseparable friends.

"That man you see there would give his life for you, without blinking, and you're pushing him away from you, just because you refuse to believe he's really found the woman for him. She isn't what you think she is. Your fear of losing James over her has made you turn that tiny possibility into a certainty."

Once more, the old man dragged him to another scene, one he had feared ever since this damn nightmare had started--the night he had discovered Rose in bed with the engineer in charge of one of his ongoing constructions.

She wanted more than she thought he could give her, more money, more luxury, and more status. She had been his first love, his first submissive and he had believed she felt the same. But she only saw him as a way out of her sad life in the low-class neighborhoods where she was born. She wasn't even really into BDSM, which had been a lie, too.

"Remember her?" the old man asked, in a mocking tone.

Alec frowned. "How could I forget?" he remembered the yelling, the accusations, the truths ventilated and how insecure he had felt for a while after that. He had also been furious with himself for not being able to see the truth sooner.

"Well, you should have, because she was an irrelevant episode in your life that you allowed to become the center of it, the yardstick by which you measure every woman who comes into your life. You keep them all at a safe distance from you, because you think they'll all turn out to be another Rose."

"How can you say she was irrelevant? I…"

"Before you finish that sentence, think about it a little. Was your heart really hurt when she left? Or just your pride? Did you or did you not hold on to that episode to avoid getting too close to a woman, and being abandoned like your mother abandoned you?"

Enraged, Alec looked at the old man, clasping his hands in tight fists. But the words were out and he couldn't stop thinking about them. Had he really loved her? He looked at the scene once more, the way they were fighting, and he had to admit he didn't seem to have a broken heart, just a bruised pride.

"Another thing you should have in mind: Hannah is not Rose. They couldn't be more different," the old man added, in a scolding tone.

Alec was hearing the old man's voice, but his mind was still swirling with doubts, refusing to take these visions as something real and not just products of his mind, in a vain wish to change things.

The old man made him fall over the bed in the dungeon.

"Not all people have the chance to get another perspective on their lives. Don't waste yours." His words sounded as a warning. "The Spirit of the Present will be visiting you soon." And those were his last words before disappearing in thin air.

Alec opened his eyes to the sound of the alarm clock on his cell phone, somewhere in the dungeon.

He got up in bed and immediately remembered the dream, because it had to be a dream. He looked at his thigh and a red welt marked the tanned skin. He looked at it for a few seconds before his rational mind came up with an explanation; he'd surely hit himself with the whip while he had been practicing. Yes, that was what had happened.

Despite that, he was unable to get the damn dream out of his mind.

Chapter Nine

Katherine spent the whole week on tenterhooks. Her body was eager to go back to the club and finally experience all he had promised her, but her mind was still a bit upset with the way the night had ended the last time.

But, this time her body overpowered her mind, and on Saturday evening, she was there at the club's door.

The guard, John, opened the door for her with a welcoming smile, walking her to the coat room before leading her to the main room.

"You can find Sir Alec near the bar, Miss Katherine," he informed her, leaving her at the door. She took a look at the crowded room, and taking a deep breath, she entered, walking to where John had shown her.

Alec was there, leaning on the bar, looking at the door. He spotted her immediately, but didn't move a muscle.

She slowly walked up to him, stopping a few feet from him.

"Good evening, girl." He greeted her with an amused smile.

"Good evening," she answered, twisting her hands, one on the other. She had no idea how he expected her to act.

"Ready for me?" he asked with a devious smile.

"I have no idea what are you going to do to me, so it's a bit hard to get ready for that, wouldn't you say?" she asked, sarcastically.

The deviousness of his smile became more obvious, but he didn't utter a word. He closed the distance between them and cradling her face, he claimed her lips with a deep kiss that left her breathless.

Taking her by the hand, he guided to the same corridor he had taken her the week before, this time only stopping when they reached a door, and he opened it for her.

The room was decorated in shades of deep red. Its main feature was the huge canopy bed, and to complete it, there were a cross and a couple of different benches scattered around the room.

"Do you like it?" he asked, walking in and stopping behind her. His hands slid to her chest cupping her breasts with both his hands.

"Yes, it's amazing," she answered, not sure she was referring to the room or to what she felt each time he laid his hands on her.

He laid a few kisses and nibbles on her ear and neck, before he released her and faced her.

"Good. Do you know what a safe word is?" he asked, going straight to business.

"Yes, of course," she answered, offended by the question.

"Do you have one?" he asked, ignoring her tone.

"No, I've never had to use one," she admitted. She hadn't done much of anything.

"The club's safe word is RED, so use it if you need to. I'm assuming you know when to use it," he said, in a presumptuous tone that almost, just almost, made her walk out the door.

"Yes, when you become a bigger badass than you already are," she answered, unable to hold it.

He pursed his lips in disgust, but didn't say anything, regarding her remark. Right now he just wanted to have her in his hands, as his submissive.

"Good. Are you willing to start?" he asked instead.

"Yes, I believe so. What will you be doing?" she asked, wanting to know exactly what she was getting into.

"I'll start by tying you up, using some of my favorite knots, maybe use a soft flogger on you and even take you to one of the benches for some spanking. Do you think you can take it?" he asked, and his eyes had a different glow in them.

Alec had to admit he was feeling more aroused than he had expected. It would be a true challenge to stage a scene with her.

"Very well, that sounds fine," she replied, her head down, concealing her feelings. She was bit disappointed. He didn't intend to have sex with her? She knew that not all scenes ended up with sex, but she wouldn't have believed that this one would be one of those. God, she was already on fire. Her whole body felt as if she was on the very verge of the abyss.

He took a step closer to her, and with his index finger under her chin, he pulled her face up.

"The odds are we will end up engaging in sex, so if you don't want that, I need a solid 'no' right now." His eyes locked on hers. "Is it a 'no'?" She shook her head, torrents of relief rushing through her body. "Say it out loud. I don't want false interpretations," he insisted.

"It's not a 'no'," she answered, in a low voice, thrilled to see the fire burning deep inside his dark eyes.

"Good, let's start then. From now on, I want you to call me Sir. I want you to make a real effort to refrain from using that brat tongue of yours and for you to treat me with respect. You can speak freely, within limits, but don't overuse that privilege, or I might decide a nice gag would come in handy. No protests, I'm the one giving the orders here. So unless something surpasses a hard limit or what you're consenting to do now, I don't want to hear it," he said, and his voice changed completely. She would have sworn he had grown a couple of inches in front of her. His tone was deeper and his face looked as if he had dropped the mask of the civilized man and was now showing the raw, primal predator he really was.

A shudder of expectation ran down her spine, and she was only able to nod her acceptance.

"Words, I want to hear words every time I ask you something. All your answers and sentences must have a 'yes Sir' or ' no Sir' somewhere in it. Do you understand?"he asked. "Too many infractions will certainly lead to punishment. I believe you have enough knowledge of how the dynamic works, so I'm sure you understand that."

"Yes, Sir. You will take into consideration that I'm new in this, right, Sir?" she asked, trying to control the level of irony placed on the word 'Sir'.

His grin meant nothing good for her, that was for sure.

"Of course, I will take that into consideration."

"Thank you, Sir."

"Is everything clear? Can we start?" his question showed her his impatience to start, and she had to admit hers perfectly matched his.

She looked at him for a second, breathing deeply before she answered.

"Yes, Sir, I'm ready."

"Good, strip completely and leave your clothes in a neat pile over that chair," he said, signaling a chair by the door. It was his first order and he was able to see her fight her first instinct, to tell him to go straight to hell. The night was going to be something special, he was sure.

Katherine bit her bottom lip to avoid a sassy retort and slowly she started to take off her clothes and lay them neatly on the chair. During the whole time, he stood there, arms crossed over his chest, watching her every move. When the final piece of clothing, her black thong, came off, she felt the heat of a blush forming on her cheeks. She didn't remember having stood naked in front of a man like that before. It was hard not to feel self-conscious of her body.

"Are you done?" he asked, sarcastically, obviously referring to all the time she had taken just to remove her clothes.

"Yes, Sir."

"Very well." He took a step closer and grabbed her by her mane, hard, pulling her head back, in a harsh pull. "So, you were saying about me being a badass?" he asked, with a devious grin that made her dry swallow.

"Just my poorly founded opinion, Sir. I'm sure when I get to know you well, my opinion will change, Sir," she answered, her eyes locked on his, defiant, ignoring the sharp pain at her nape.

He looked at her and she could tell he was struggling between laughing and killing her. Fortunately, he decided to laugh, even if it was a short, dry laugh.

"Don't ever lose that spirit, sub," he said, loosening a bit of the pressure of his grip. He led her, by her mane toward the center of the room, leaving her there to go pick a few things from a cabinet on the other side of the room. He picked ropes and a few other items she wasn't able to see what they were.

He returned to her, picking a small table on his way where he rested all the objects. He put the table next to her and took a few more minutes to look at her body, touching here and there, setting small fires all over her, wherever he touched.

Anticipation had her on the edge, already.

He finally grabbed the rope he had chosen, a beautiful red cotton rope, strong and at the same time, soft enough to avoid rope burns.

He untied the rope, and folding it in half, he started to work, moving her body at his will, as if she was a little more than a doll.

The ropes went around her breasts, tightly, making them tense up, and though it didn't hurt yet, she could feel the pressure building inside her. After he was done with that part, he tied her arms behind her back, before he came back to her breasts, making the rope imprison her already hard nipples, applying even more pressure to the whole breast.

Her breath was getting heavier, and her heart thundered deafeningly in her chest. The feeling of his hands on her, added to the bittersweet kiss of the rope, had her completely aroused. She could feel the evidence of her desire slowly slipping through her lips.

When he was satisfied with the ropes over her breasts, he continued down, making lovely knots down her belly.

"Please, open your legs, shoulder-width," he ordered when he reached her crotch.

She hesitated, not sure she wanted him to see just how wet she was. But a single look at his face was more than enough to make her obey. He wouldn't tolerate any disobedience, and she had no intention of getting punished that night, not if she could help it.

"Yes, Sir!" and she slowly opened her legs.

With a grin, he ran his fingers through her crotch, making them slide inside her lips, and taking them out completely coated in her cream, ripping a muffled moan from her lips.

"Someone is having fun," he said, with a devious grin, cleaning her fingers on her breasts, smearing her cream all over them, before he made the ropes go through her slit, tightening them hard, making her gasp, when he pulled them from behind, sinking the rope into her tender skin, one at each side of her lips, and then two inside her lips, applying pressure to her pussy and clit. "Is there a problem, sub?"

"No, Sir, no problem," she stammered, still panting a little bit.

"Good," he replied, finishing his work with the ropes. "Are you in pain?" he asked, checking all the ties.

"Not yet, Sir," she answered, knowing that the pressure she was feeling on her breasts would soon change into a dull ache.

"That's good. Let me know if it becomes unbearable," he said, looking at her, relishing his rope work on her; the way her breasts poked, tense, gaining that purplish tone so beautiful, and the way the ropes caged her hard nipples, making them stand out, hard and proud.

"Yes, Sir," her voice was little more than a whisper, her chest was heaving, and her breathing was labored.

She was aroused and he knew it wouldn't take much to make her go over the edge, but he wanted her to hold it back, as much as he could make her do so.

He leaned over, pushed the ropes over her clit aside and started brushing his fingers over her aching knob, as he whispered in her ear:

"You can't come without permission, sub, and if you do, it will be considered a huge infraction, worthy of immediate punishment, understood?"

She whimpered at his words and actions, and his fingers never left her clit. She bit her bottom lip hard, trying to hold back the orgasm that had been building inside her, ever since she met him again.

There was no way in hell she would be able to stop it, if he kept rubbing her clit the way he was doing at that moment.

"Yes… Sir… I understand." But her legs almost failed her, due to the intense shuddering. He grabbed her by her waist with his other hand, his fingers never leaving her crotch. "Please… Sir… please…" she begged, not sure whether she wanted him to stop, or just allow her to let go. "Please, I can't take it anymore."

"What do you want, sub?" he whispered again, the tip of his tongue exploring her earlobe, making her shudder a little more.

"Let me come, please, Sir!" she begged once more, feeling the bulge of emotions spreading all over her. She wouldn't make it.

She felt a sharp smack just over her aroused clit, at the same time he bit down hard on the crook of her neck and she lost it.

She flew over the edge, the bulge exploded inside her and she simply dived, head first on an ocean of pleasure and bliss.

And she came, hard, with no permission. Her body went flaccid in his arms and he had to grab her harder to stop her from falling to the floor.

Chapter Ten

"Oh, dear, you just came," he said in her ear, and his grin told her just how pleased he was with that. She had just given him an excuse, in case he needed one, to punish her.

She slowly returned to earth from her trip to the depths of bliss.

"You did that on purpose… Sir!" she accused him. But he didn't answer her accusation. He just helped her stand steady on her feet before he released her.

"I believe I told you I didn't want to hear any protests, didn't I?" he asked, his tone colder than ever, as he pushed the ropes back into place, viciously tugging them over her clit.

"Yes, Sir!" she mumbled, gasping, the shot of pain rushing through her body.

"Did you or did you not disobey my order?" he asked her again.

"Yes Sir, I did," she admitted, struggling with the huge desire of kicking him in the ass. Maybe she wasn't cut out to be a submissive, after all.

"Did I or did I not tell you not to come without permission? And that if you did, you would be punished?" he asked again, and she felt her rage reach even higher levels.

"Yes, Sir, you did. What you didn't say was that you would do all in your power to make me come, and that's unfair," she added, unable to hold her tongue.

He almost laughed. He was poking her, just to see what kind of submissive she was. And though she had behaved so beautifully while he was tying her, he had known the whole time she was a real shrew, and that it would show up sooner or later. But instead of being displeased, he liked her strong spirit. She was a very strong woman, even while submitting.

"A second protest, your punishments are starting to pile up."

She looked at him and he could see all the rage she had inside. The best part was, despite all that, she still wasn't calling red.

Katherine bit her lips hard to stop herself from adding even more punishments. She wanted so much to wipe that hideous smile off his face with a good, old punch.

"Anything else to add?" he asked, teasing her.

"No, Sir!" she answered between clenched teeth.

"Good. Let's proceed then to your punishment." He announced and she couldn't help shuddering a bit.

She had never been punished in her life. Her parents had never laid a hand on her, not because they were loving parents, just because they were never around long enough for that. So she had no idea how she was going to feel about it. She had witnessed many punishment scenes in all the clubs she had been to in the past year, and she had felt aroused seeing them, but she had no idea how it would feel on her own skin or if she would be able to take it.

"What are you going to do, Sir?" she asked, apprehensively. "I've never done this before, so I have no idea of what to expect," she admitted.

"Not more than you can take, I'm sure, but if you feel it's too much, call red and we'll discuss it," he answered his tone blatant.

"Discuss? I thought calling red would end things completely," she said, puzzled.

"Only if you want to stop, otherwise, we'll discuss whatever is bothering you and decide if we should continue or not," he explained patiently. "But, if you call red by whim, I'll be the one ending it all. I have no time to waste with fakes. You have to be dedicated to this as much as I am; even when it comes to receiving your punishments."

"I see," she said, having trouble combining the two sides of him, the cold-hearted badass and the considerate dominant.

"And I believe we can add another punishment to your list. If I'm not mistaken, it's been three times now you failed to address me correctly."

She looked at him, failing to understand what he was saying until flashes of the three mentioned times came to her mind and she moaned, frustrated.

"Yes, Sir!"

"Let's start then," he grabbed her by her hair again, and led her to one of the spanking benches. It had a support for her legs, so she was going to be kneeling over it, her legs spread and her torso bending over the bench, exposing her ass to him. Her hands were already tied at her back, so he fastened a strap of leather over her mid back to ensure she wouldn't be able to get up.

She was panting hard, nervousness and anticipation rushing through her at a maddening pace.

"Since it's your first time, I'll warm you up a bit before I get to the punishment itself. It will be easier on you," he said, but for her it was as if he was talking Chinese. "Ready?"

"Yes Sir!"

He stood beside the bench, with full access to her whole body and then he ran his hand over her buttocks a couple of times before he started to smack them.

He started with light smacks, just teasers, as he hit every inch of her ass, but slowly he increased the strength of the blows until he reached a point where every single blow stung like hell and her whimpers were loud and clear. She was sure her buttocks would be completely red.

He stopped, his hands again caressing her reddened skin, his fingers sliding through her slit, finding her still wet, and he was sure she was even wetter than before.

Katherine was gasping for air. She was making a huge effort not to cry in front of him, but she knew she wouldn't hold on much longer. When he slid his finger down her slit, the moan that came out of her mouth had nothing to do with pain. It was of sheer pleasure, and she felt as a wave of pleasure wash over her whole body.

He stepped back and grabbed a black leather paddle from a cabinet nearby and showed it to her.

"I'll give you fifteen strokes: ten for coming without permission and five for being disrespectful," he announced to her and she closed her eyes, not sure she could bear it. Her buttocks already hurt a lot. "And I'm being kind here, because it's your first time; otherwise, I would be using my cane, at least thirty times, so be thankful," he added, in that cold tone she was starting to hate.

"Yes, Sir," she accepted.

He smacked her hard with the paddle, filling her eyes with tears.

"I said 'be thankful'," he repeated his order, "and this one doesn't count."

She sobbed and managed to mumble, "Thank you Sir." But he could sense her rage. Her spirit was still high. "You're such a considered Dom, Sir."

Away from her eyes, he smiled a broad, pleased, smile. That was his girl.

"Since you are so talkative now, I want you to count every blow, and thank me for each one of them," he decided at the last moment, wanting her to feel so enraged that the pain would go by more easily. "Are we clear, sub?"

"Yes, Sir."

"Good!"

And the first blow came down hard, over her left buttock, and she muffled a small cry, pressing her mouth to the bench.

"One, Sir, thank you," she said through gritted teeth.

The second one fell over her right cheek and again she managed to hide her cry.

"Two, Sir, thank you."

And three, four, five. And he stopped. His hand caressed the offended skin, appeasing some of the pain, and she even sensed something that felt like soft kisses, but she discarded that idea as inconceivable.But he was indeed kissing her, relishing the redness of her skin, the welts left by his own hand. Once more, he slid his fingers through her slit, brushing them all over her pussy, taking special care with her clit, rubbing it, pressing it hard until he heard her moan, her hands clasping hard.

And it started again, six, seven, eight, nine, ten, and by then, she had tears running down her cheeks, her buttocks were on fire, and she wanted to kill him for making her thank him for it.

He stopped again, once more caressing her skin, appeasing the pain and making sure she felt even more aroused, teasing her clit until he heard her whimper with pleasure.

The eleventh blow came, and this time she wasn't able to stop it.

She screamed at the stinging.

"Eleven, Sir… thank you," she shouted, sobbing even more.

"Do you want to call red, sub?" he asked, but he knew she wouldn't. She was hurting, but he was sure she could take that and so much more.

"No, Sir, I don't," she answered, through gritted teeth again.

"We will have to discuss that bad habit you seem to have of talking through gritted teeth," he admonished her, and she wished she could use those teeth to bite him hard, no matter where.

"Yes, Sir!" she answered.

The twelfth blow landed, and she cried even harder.

"Twelve, Sir… thank you," she said through sobs.

The thirteenth blow came fast after that, and she could almost swear it wasn't as hard as the last ones, but that couldn't be right, could it? He wouldn't go easy on her.

"Thirteen, Sir… thank you," she shouted again, closing her eyes, telling herself she had to be insane to accept this, to go through all this pain, just because she had contravened some stupid rules.

The last two landed in a fast mode, not allowing her to count them separately.

"Fourteen and fifteen, Sir... thank you," she said, sobbing a bit less, sighing with relief when he dropped the damned paddle to the floor.

"Good girl!" The pleasure was obvious in his tone. Her face was red, her eyes swollen, her cheeks drenched in tears, but those two little words had the power to make her feel better than if she had just won the biggest prize in the universe, and she sighed with pleasure.

Chapter Eleven

Katherine felt him fuss behind her, and she felt the ropes around her pussy get loosened, and then completely removed. She was still bent over the bench, and she could feel him now behind her, between her spread legs.

He caressed her sore skin once more, running his fingers over the welts, hearing her whimper beneath his touch, before he went down on her, kissing her skin, licking it, making some of the pain go away.

His fingers went back to her sore pussy, now freed of the ropes, rubbing it, poking her entrance and teasing her clit, enjoying the obvious change on the tone of her sobs.

He entered her with one of his fingers, in a single thrust, caressing her inner walls, feeling the shudders of her body.

She was so ready for him, and his shaft was so hard, he no longer could hold back. He removed his fingers from her, smiling at her moans of protest, and unzipped his pants, finally releasing his hard cock from its imprisonment.

He grabbed her by her buttocks, running his cock up and down her slit, smearing it in her cream. Then he rammed it in, hard and deep, feeling, for the first time, the wild pleasure of her walls welcoming him, clenching around him as he stretched her.

In and out, he shoved himself, matching his growls with her moans, knowing he wouldn't last long.

Katherine gasped as he entered her, pain from her smacks mixing with the incredible pleasure of feeling him buried inside her, feeling her body shudder more and more, and she knew she was going to come again.

"Please… Sir, please!" she begged.

"Are you ready for me, sub? Are you ready to come for me?" he asked her, his breath labored

"Yes, Sir, Yes!"

He growled once more before he ordered her:

"Then come with me, do it!"

And her body simply obeyed. The pleasure building inside her exploded in wild waves of pleasure that threw her over the edge, taken by him into a fantastic dimension where only pleasure and bliss existed.

Feeling her shudder and quiver underneath him, the way her walls clenched hard around him and her cries of pleasure was more than he could take so he let himself go, pouring his essence deep inside her, as his body was taken by powerful shudders.

He leaned his head back, taking a deep breath as his body slowly came back to normal. That had been one of the most powerful experiences he had ever had.

Katherine had her eyes closed, still panting, her heart drumming in her chest. She had gotten her answer. That was why she was there. She had never experienced something like what had just happened between Alec and her. And she wasn't talking just about the physical pleasure. Incredibly, they had managed to create a strong bond between them, that had taken the experience to a higher level, a level she didn't even know existed. Everything was worth it for living something like this. Everybody should live it at least once in their lives.

Alec let his cock slide out of her drenched pussy, watching, pleased as their mixed juices slowly came out of her, rolling down her inner thighs.

Carefully, he released her from the bench and carried her to the bed, laying her there, her golden mane spread over the burgundy sheets, her eyes closed, and an expression of bliss on her face that only made him feel more pleased.

Slowly he started to remove the ropes from her body, relishing every ligature mark printed in her ivory skin. She only moaned of displeasure when blood rushed back to her breasts, but it only lasted a moment.

He lay in bed next to her, and pulled her towards him, making her rest her head in the crook of his arm.

"Are you alright, sub?" he asked his voice with a rare warm tone.

She opened her eyes slightly, just to make sure she wasn't delirious, amazed to see the pleased smile on his face.

"Yes, I'm alright, Sir," she admitted.

"Do you think you want to learn more? Experience more?" he asked, his fingers trailing the rope marks on her breasts.

"Yes, I'm sure I want to, Sir," she answered, sighing.

"Do you think you'll still feel the same when you try to sit later and your lovely buttocks hurt like hell?" he asked, half teasing, half serious.

She snorted, furious.

"I'm not that shallow," she replied. A hard smack landed on her back thigh. "Hey!"

"Don't snort at me, and you forgot again," he explained, with a devious smile on his face. "I can see punishments will be a regular event between us."

"Only because you're a sadistic Dom, Sir," she answered, furious.

"Yes, I am, I'm a sadist, and you my dear have more of a masochist inside you than you ever thought possible," he answered, sure of his words. Despite all the pain he knew she had gone through, her arousal had never diminished, and he was sure he could train her to endure more, much more.

"No, I'm sure you're wrong. I hated every second of that punishment… Sir," she retorted.

"Time will prove me right. And adding it like that won't work," he said, referring to her last minute addition of the word Sir.

"Yes, Sir," she said, after discreetly showing him her tongue.

"I saw that, and that's the second time I've caught you doing that, sub," he said, and though his tone was amused, she was sure he wouldn't forget it and she would have to pay for it.

"I'm so sorry, Sir." But her tone made it clear she wasn't.

"The night is still young, and tonight we're having some performances here at the club. Would you like to stick around to see them?" he invited

her, wanting to keep her with him for a while
longer.

"What kind of performances?" she asked,
curious.

"We'll have a couple of riggers, a Dom
experienced with fireplay, another one that is an
expert in knifeplay, and yet another that works
beautifully with needles," he informed her.

"Wow, that's heavy stuff, Sir."

"Yes, but believe me, it's a lifetime experience to
see these guys working." He pulled her chin up,
making her face him. "Do you want to stay?"

"Yes, I would love to, Sir."

"I'll expect you to act as my sub the whole time,"
he warned her.

"And what does that mean, exactly, Sir?" she
asked, puzzled.

"You'll be respectful at all times. If I sit, you'll
kneel next to me. You won't talk unless I ask you
something, and if someone else talks to you, you
must always ask for my permission to answer
them," he told her.

"Really? Are you serious, Sir?" she couldn't but
help.

"I'm not a high protocol master, but I am very strict. I have my own rules, and I expect them to be followed blindly; no protests will be tolerated," he confirmed he was dead serious. "If you think it's too much for you, I want to know it now."

She looked at him and considered her options. Was she willing to do all that just to be with him? Was he worth all that trouble? She didn't have much knowledge of BDSM protocols, but she was aware that high protocol didn't stray far from the total objectification of the submissive. He had said he didn't go that far, but he sure was way stricter than any other Dom she had met in the past year.

But, the truth was she had been feeling a bit disappoint those last weeks, for not being able to find someone that met her expectations. So far, Alec had surpassed them, even the wildest ones.

"Will you teach me what you want me to do, Sir? Or do you plan to punish me for making mistakes I'm not aware of?" she asked, because she had no intention to become his boxing bag.

"Have I done that to you?" he asked in a cold tone.

"No, Sir, I just want to make things clear between us," she answered, sincerely.

"Very well, I'll always tell you in advance what I expect from you. But once warned, there's no suitable excuse," he added.

"Yes, Sir, then, I agree to stay."

"I'll make you wear a temporary collar, since I want everyone to know that you're taken. It's not a real collar, just something for you to wear whenever we are here at the club," he announced, jumping out of bed.

"Thank you, Sir."

"Come join me in the shower. We need to get you cleaned up and ready for the rest of the night," he said, stretching out his hand, offering her support. She grabbed his hand and let him pull her out of bed.

He took her to a huge shower where he dedicated the following minutes to carefully washing her body, taking special care with her very sore buttocks.

"Does it hurt too much?" he asked, when she moaned while he was soaping her ass cheeks.

She thought about it before she answered his question. Yes, she felt the burning sensation on her ass, and she was sure she would hurt when she sat on it, but it wasn't that bad. Her moan had more than pain in it, but she still wasn't ready to admit that.

"No Sir, not too much," she answered.

"Good girl," he replied, with a wicked smile. "Your turn to wash me, girl," he ordered, handing her the bathing cloth.

She took it gladly, taking the chance to explore his fantastic body, running her soapy fingers over his hard muscles.

When she reached his cock, she hesitated, but he encouraged her to go on, taking her hand in his and guiding it there. She washed it thoroughly, loving the way his cock reacted to her touch, the way it grew underneath her hand.

He moaned, pleased, and she smiled.

"It seems I'll need some help, now, girl," he said, resting his hands on her shoulders and pushing her gently to her knees, presenting her his hard, fat cock.

She didn't hesitate. She grabbed him with her hands and taking her tongue out, she flipped its tip all over his head, enjoying the softness of its skin, its bittersweet taste before she took the head into her mouth, sucking hard, eager to feel that first drop of nectar flooding her mouth with exquisite flavor, and she wasn't disappointed.

He pushed himself a bit further into her mouth, showing her his impatience, and she took him deeper, sucking harder, helping herself with her hands, stroking him and playing with his balls.

He growled, and taking her by her mane, he ordered:

"Hands behind your back girl."

She obeyed, and he proceeded to shove his cock in and out of her mouth at a much faster pace, sometimes making her gag, but never stopping until he erupted against the back of her throat, with an animalistic growl, his body quivering hard.

He pulled her up, still with threads of his cum rolling down the corners of her mouth, being washed away by the warm stream of water from the shower.

He cradled her face between his hands and claimed a passionate kiss from her lips, tasting his own flavor on her.

After that, they finished bathing and he made her return to the bedroom wrapped in a huge white towel.

"I want you to wait here for me. I'll get you some clothes to wear, as well as a collar. Don't open the door to anyone else," he warned her.

"Yes, Sir."

When he left the room, she combed her hair with a comb she found in a drawer and then lay back in bed, looking at the dark red canopy as she processed all that had happened since she had met him, astonished that it hadn't even been twenty-four hours. What kind of spell was she under that made her put herself completely in the hands of a stranger? Yes, a stranger that she felt as if she had known all her life, but still, a stranger. She didn't even know his last name, where he lived, what he did for a living, nothing.

Did it matter? She had to be honest with herself and admit it didn't, not in that particular moment.

Chapter Twelve

The door opened, and he entered. He threw her a small, black piece of fabric that she discovered was supposed to be a dress.

She extended it in front of her, doubting her curves would fit in it.

"Don't you think that's too small for me, Sir?" she asked, with a frown.

"I'm sure it will fit perfectly. Put it on," he answered, with a naughty smile.

"Did you get me some underwear, Sir?" she asked, still doubtful.

"You won't need it." His tone stated clearly that he wouldn't allow any discussion on the subject.

She got out of bed and put on the dress. The fabric stretched and the thing, she couldn't even call it a dress, fit like a damn glove, enhancing all her curves, making her nipples stand out, hard as they were, only covering half her thighs.

"Perfect, I knew you would look beautiful in it," he said when she was done.

"This is indecent, Sir!" she spurted, and it only made him grin even more.

"Perfect, like I said. Put on your sandals. All the shoes I was able to find were too high for you hurt feet," he ordered again, and she complied. "Now, please kneel in front of me."

"Yes, Sir." She looked at him, curious, but did as told. She knelt in front of him.

"Hold your hair up." It was his next order, and she realized what he was going to do, and a million butterflies took flight inside her stomach. He was going to collar her, and even when she knew it wasn't the real thing, it felt pretty much like it.

He leaned forward and wrapped the black leather collar around her neck, buckling it in place. The noise of the buckle sounding ominous in the silence of the room.

Alec buckled the collar around her neck, telling himself it didn't mean anything, that it was just a collar for her to wear at the club, with no meaning other than a needed accessory. But, strangely, he wasn't convincing himself.

"There, you're ready," he said, lifting her chin with two fingers and kissing her hard and deep, until they were both gasping for air.

He finally helped her up, and taking a leash out of his pocket, he hooked it to her collar.

Katherine looked at it, astonished.

"A leash… Sir? Really?" she asked in shock, almost forgetting to address him.

"A leash, girl, do you have a problem with it?" his question, in a tone capable of creating droplets of ice from thin air, told her it wasn't a good idea to discuss this with him, so she shook her head.

"No, Sir, no problem."

"Good girl." He had expected a great deal of protest from her, but, obviously, he hadn't measured well her desire to do this, to be there, and that pleased him in a way he wasn't able to explain, not even to himself. "Let's go then. Remember the few rules I gave you and we'll be just fine."

"Yes, Sir," she answered with a grimace. Rules, she was starting to hate the word.

He took her back to the main room of the club, approaching a small table with a little sign on it reading 'Reserved', just in front of the main stage. He sat down and she was going to kneel next to him, but he didn't let her.

"This time, take a seat on a chair. I want you to have a good view of the stage, since I would like to try with you some of the things you'll be seeing here," he said, signaling the chair next to him.

She sat down carefully, feeling her buttocks hurt like she was sitting on embers.

But only a few moments after that, the first performance started, and she was able to put her discomfort in the back of her mind. It was a well-renowned rigger, who showed a few really amazing suspensions, and the bond between him and his bottom was amazing.

The next one was the expert in fireplay and Katherine told herself she would never let anyone do that to her. It looked way too dangerous and the thought of having real fire dancing over her body was more than she could take. Even so, the performance was impressive, especially when you looked at the submissive's face and saw just how serene she was.

The one that followed was the needle lover, a femme dome. And this time, Katherine experienced mixed feelings watching it. First, she drew an intricate figure with several needles, of different sizes and colors over her submissive's shoulder blade; then, she moved to her breasts. She showed the audience some needles at least five inches long, before she proceeded to cross the other woman's nipple, from one side to the other, and repeated the process with the other four needles, forming a star.

Katherine looked at the scene completely mesmerized. Her whole body shuddered, but she just couldn't keep her eyes away from it. Her brain kept telling her that what she was seeing was insane, but her body was having a very confusing response. She was panting, her heart pounded hard against her chest, and she was starting to realize that Alec could be right to some degree when he said she thrilled by pain.

She watched the whole performance, staring at the stage.

"What did you think of that?" There was the question she would have loved not to answer.

"That's insane, Sir," she answered, using her brain's opinion. She wasn't sharing the rest, not with him.

"Are you sure that's all you think of it?" he asked again, drawing closer to her, so much so, that she could feel his breath brushing her ear.

"Yes, Sir, just that," she insisted. She would only admit anything else under torture.

He cupped her face, and made her face him, his eyes locked on hers.

"I can smell your arousal, girl. So, I'm going to ask you again, and I better get the truth this time; what did you think of it?" His tone was cold and carried a promise more than a threat.

"I really think it's insane, Sir, but at the same time, it appeals to me in ways that I don't seem to quite understand," she finally said, closing her eyes for a moment, not wanting to believe she had admitted that.

He brushed his lips over hers, in a light caress, before he assailed her mouth in a deep, powerful kiss that claimed his ownership over her, to all around them.

They finished watching the other performances, like the knifeplay, but none other had the same effect on her.

It was midnight when the performances ended, and the night was still young. He took her around the room and to the dungeons, showing her everything, answering all her questions with a patience she hadn't thought he possessed.

By around two in the morning, they had seen practically everything there was to be seen, they had talked to several of his friends, and the night had been a dream come true for her.

He whispered in her ear, "Let's go back to the room, I want you." The order, the hoarseness of his tone, almost melted her right there and then, and meekly, she followed him, more than willing.

He opened the door for her to enter and as soon as she stepped inside, one of his big hands flew right to her neck, smashing her against the wall next to the door, kissing her until he left her breathless.

He unzipped his pants, freeing his hard cock, pulled up one of her legs, exposing her drenched pussy, and before she could take another breath, he was thrusting himself inside her, hard, fast, and deep.

His mouth was glued to the crook of her neck, and his teeth sank into the tender flesh as he plunged in and out of her, creating a frenzy of emotions inside her, dragging her fast to the edge.

"Please… Sir, oh, god, please…" she begged, as the sensations overwhelmed her so fast and so deep.

"Do you want to come, girl? Want to come for me?" he asked, and again his voice was unrecognizable, hoarse and deep, as if he was containing too many emotions, inside him.

"Yes… please… Sir…" she answered barely able to articulate the words.

"Then come with me, now," he ordered, as his body shuddered wildly, pushing her with him over the edge, torrents of pleasure running over their bodies, leaving no inch untouched.

He collapsed over her, pushing her even more against the wall, staying there for a few moments before he took her to bed, still buried inside her until he laid her there, helping her out of her dress and leash and getting rid of his own clothes before he lay next to her, cuddling her to his body, kissing her all over her shoulders and neck.

"I hope you had a good time tonight," he whispered in her ear.

"Yes, Sir, the best, thank you."

"Are you willing to do it again?" he asked, killing the doubt that had started to worry her.

"Yes, Sir, I am," she answered.

"Good girl. That being so, I want you to meet me here next Saturday, at seven pm," he demanded. "Meanwhile, you're not allowed to date any other man, and if you have any kind of relationship you ought to finish it as soon as possible."

Chapter Thirteen

She hadn't dated in quite some time, but even so, his tone just pushed her beyond her limits.

"So, I have to become a nun for a week, Sir? Are you going to do the same, or does this rule only apply to me, Sir?" she asked, the word 'sir' oozing sarcasm all over it, as she rolled away from him to look him straight in the face.

He looked at her, his expression again that hideous stone-carved mask.

"The rule applies to both of us. No outsiders, I'm not poly, and I don't like to share what's mine," he answered, cold as ice. "I'm sure you can go a week without getting laid."

She snorted at the rude expression.

"I don't get laid, Sir."

He rolled over on the bed, pinning her down by her neck, his whole body over hers, immobilizing her completely.

"I believe I already told you not to snort at me," he said slowly, word by word, as his hand applied more pressure to her neck, sinking her collar into her skin.

She could feel her air supply grow shorter, and her chest heaved to get more air in. But strangely, she wasn't afraid, her hands not even moving to try and take his hand from her neck.

Her eyes locked on his, her face an open book for him, her trust in him touching a part of his soul he had believed to be completely dead.

Slowly, he loosened his grip, without removing his hand completely, leaning his head down, kissing her fiercely, their argument completely forgotten under the strength of the passion they shared.

Voracious kisses and wild caresses raised their arousal once more, and soon he was hard again, craving to make her his once more.

He flipped her over, getting her on all fours, as he grabbed her by her hips with both hands and he shoved himself deep inside her, growling at her deep moan. Then he took her mane with one of his hands, pulling hard, making her head lean back, as he moved in and out of her, plunging himself, dragging her with him once more through the trails of the wildest pleasure they had ever experienced.

When calm was restored, she collapsed over the bed, her body completely drained, and her eyes closed as she fell deeply asleep.

Alec looked at her, with a devious smile. Apparently, he had left her exhausted. He lay beside her and carefully pulled her closer to him, laying her head on his chest before he, too, fell asleep.

Katherine opened her eyes, feeling disoriented. She was alone in bed and Alec was nowhere to be seen. She got up and went to the bathroom for a quick shower, removing her collar before she did. Somehow, it felt awful to take it off, which was nonsense, but she just couldn't shake the feeling. She left it, placed carefully on top of the dress she had worn the night before, the tips of her fingers lingering over it, reluctant to leave it there.

She had no idea what time was it, but it was morning according to the position of the sun in the sky.

She put on her own clothes and decided to go home. She had no idea where he could be, but she figured it was time for her to go home.

She left the club after receiving weird looks from all the staff she came upon, and headed home immediately.

She was just getting home when she received the call. It was an unknown number, but she answered anyway. She had the feeling she knew who it was.

"Hello?" she said.

"*Why did you left like that?*" he barked on the other side.

"Good morning to you, too, Sir! Did you sleep well?" she answered back, ignoring his rudeness.

"*Answer my question, girl!*" he barked once more.

She sighed, and decided not to exasperate him even more.

"You weren't around, Sir, so I thought I was supposed to leave," she answered patiently.

"We didn't finish our conversation yesterday," he said, returning to his cold, controlled self.

"And whose fault was that, Sir?" she asked, fearless.

"I have an excellent memory, girl. Are you sure you want to go down that road?" he warned her, and she shuddered.

"No, Sir," she assured him.

"Good. So, will you come next Saturday?" he asked.

"Yes, Sir, I'll be there. Will I be allowed to enter? After all, I'm not a member there," she asked, curious.

"But I am, and I've added your name as my guest," he informed her. "Remember the rules and we'll meet next Saturday."

"What if I get too horny, Sir? Can I take care of that by myself?" she asked, to annoy him more than anything else.

"No, you can't masturbate. I'm sure you can hold it for a week. It will be a good exercise for you," he answered in that same cold tone.

"Yes, Sir, I'm sure it will. See you next week, Sir."

"See you then, girl."

She ended the call and looked at her phone for a few moments. The man could be so damn irritating.

The week went by in a blur filled with anxiety, anticipation, and so many other mixed feelings. Sooner than she would have wanted, Saturday arrived. Unlike herself, she hadn't told Lucy anything about Alec. Things were too new, too fresh, and she just felt she should keep it to herself.

During the taxi ride to the club, her mind was swirling, imagining thousands of scenarios, considering millions of different possibilities and as soon as she set foot in the main room and her eyes met his, everything vanished, and the only thing she could think of was him.

She walked towards the table where he was waiting for her.

"Good evening, girl," he greeted her.

"Good evening, Sir," she answered back.

"From now on I don't want to see you come in those doors without having your collar on," he warned her. "I've personalized the one you wore last week, adding a few details, and I want you to take it home with you," he informed her handing her the collar for her to see.

He had engraved in the black leather the words 'Master Alec' and in the shackle he had added a silver heart with the word 'Owned' also engraved. "Do you like it?" he asked.

"I thought you said this was just a needed accessory… Sir," she recalled, unsure of what to think of the collar.

"It is, but there's no reason for it to be an ordinary collar," he answered in a cold tone. "Get on your knees and hold your hair up," he ordered, ending the subject.

She kneeled in front of him and lifted her hair high. Though this was the second time he'd buckled the collar around her neck, the feeling was the same, intense, powerful and a sense of belonging.

When he was done, he caressed her face, and ordered her to drop her hair.

"I just can't believe what I just saw. Master Iceberg Alec is taking another naive submissive under his power." The words came from the same beautiful reddish they had met last week, Hannah, he had called her. "Do you know, sweetheart, this man is a cold, empty shell, with no feelings for anyone, not even his so-called friends?" she asked, turning to Katherine. "You should leave while you can, because sooner or later you will; they all do. It's impossible to feel good around an iceberg all the time."

"Hannah, I believe you've said enough." Alec said, getting up, towering over the woman, but she wasn't easily impressed.

"Well, I believe I'll never be able to say enough. This should be one of the happiest times of James' life, but it isn't because he feels he has lost his best friend and doesn't seem to be able to understand that he's so much better off without you around," she retorted, obviously furious.

Katherine, followed the discussion, was a bit worried. She had noticed Alec's attitude when they had met the couple the week before.

"I'm not responsible for whatever your husband feels. So please, leave us alone, you're disturbing my guest," he said, in a very cold tone.

"What in the hell is going on here?" James appeared next to Hannah.

"Your wife is disturbing my guest. Maybe you could remind her of the house's rules and urge her to behave more like the submissive that she's supposed to be," Alec answered, cold as ice, his look harder than stone.

James, looked at him, and shook his head, "Don't worry; we won't cross your path again. Consider my membership terminated as of today. Have a good night." He turned to Hannah taking her by her hand. "Let's go, Hannah."

The woman looked at Alec, pain shining in her eyes, as she shook her head and walked away.

Alec turned to Katherine and helped her up.

"Let's go to one of the private rooms," he told her.

"Why…" she started to ask, but he interrupted her immediately.

Chapter Fourteen

"I don't discuss my private life with anyone." She looked at him, incredulous with the way he cut her off so brusquely. "Do you have a problem with that? We can end this right here and right now."

She considered it, or at least she tried, but she didn't want to end it, not now anyway. She had no idea of what problem he had with the other couple, and it really wasn't any of her business.

"No Sir, I have no problem with that."

"Good." He hooked her leash and drove her downstairs. As in the main floor, there was a huge room that looked pretty much like a medieval dungeon, with all kinds of crosses, benches, spider webs made of rope, hooks, and suspension gears, chains, the whole thing. Most of the devices were being used by a small crowd, but he didn't stop. He just walked right through it to another staircase that took them down to another floor. At the bottom of the stairs there was a long corridor with several doors on each side of it. All of them had name tags on it and she was able to read in the dim light some of the names: Desert Fantasy, Doctor's Office, Chapel…

He stopped in front of one that read 'Medieval Torture' and she shuddered.

He opened the door and invited her in. She took a step in and the room lightened, showing her a small version of the room on the upper floor. She looked at him, but his expression was plain.

"Please remove all your clothes, girl," he ordered, his voice very cold.

"Yes Sir."

She got undressed, standing with just her collar on.

"I'll be showing you my own version of the positions I'll ask you to adopt whenever we are together," he informed her. "Pay attention since I don't intend to repeat them and failure to adopt them will result in immediate punishment."

"You're really a sadist, aren't you, Sir?" she asked, not sure she could manage that fact.

"You could say I have a sadist vein, but I don't get a thrill out of just pain. I like to look at the way a masochist reacts to pain and to be the one inflicting that pain, but if you're talking about causing pain in a regular person, who just feels pain, for the pleasure of causing that pain, then I would say I'm not. Of course, it's different when we're talking about imposing discipline or applying punishment, then it's a duty that I, as a Master, take very seriously," he explained and she believed him and that made her feel a bit better with the whole idea.

"I see, Sir."

"I'm sure that deep within you hides a masochist, my dear, and when you're ready to accept that, you will ask for pain, you'll need it." He added, with a condescending smile.

"I might decide consciously never to accept it, Sir," she said, wanting to wipe the damn smile from his arrogant face.

"You won't be able to deny your true nature, girl," he assured her.

She snorted, and as soon as the derogatory sound came out of her mouth, she realized she had made a big mistake.

"Snorting at me again, girl? See what I mean? You do like pain," he said with a malicious smile.

"No, Sir, I assure you, I don't," she replied. But she didn't apologize and by the shine in his eyes she knew he was aware of that, and that she had no intention of doing it.

"I'll take care of that later," he promised her, and she quivered but remained firm. "Now, as for the positions, the first one is the waiting position. I want you to kneel on the floor, buttocks over your ankles, hands crossed behind your back, head lowered, looking down until I tell you otherwise. Show me."

She followed his instructions, and stayed there, still. She could sense his intense look on her.

"Very well, girl. The next one is the inspection position. Stand up, hands behind you neck, legs spread, and breasts sticking out, head up, looking forward. Show me this one as well."

She complied, and he took the opportunity to inspect her, examining thoroughly her breasts, weighing them, kneading them, squeezing them hard.

"Are they natural, girl?" he asked, just to confirm.

"Thankfully, yes, Sir, or I'd have to run to the E.R. with a possible leak," she answered, with a grimace, referring to his rough treatment.

"Girl, that mouth of yours will certainly give me much amusement, but I doubt you'll feel the same," he said chuckling.

She bit her lips hard to stop any other smart retort from coming out, and he laughed even more.

He continued with his inspection, looking for any marks from the past week, but there were none.

"Did you have any trouble last week with bruises?" he asked, running his big hand over her soft skin.

"No, Sir, by Monday morning I practically didn't feel them," she said, exaggerating the truth. She had felt sore at least until Thursday, but she had no intention of admitting that.

"Oh, good, that means I can go harder on you."

"What?! No, I mean… Sir, it was hard enough, I assure you," she mumbled, scolding herself for lying to him.

"I can read you like a book, girl, so don't even try to lie to me, or hide things from me. I'll know," he advised her.

She looked at him with disbelief, but she was not willing to put that to the test; not then, anyway.

"Yes, Sir."

"Has anyone ever used a flogger on you?" he asked, picking one from a cabinet on the other wall. This one was black, and appeared to be made of soft suede.

"No, Sir, never."

He brought it to her, running its soft strings over her body.

"Very well, that's what I'll be doing today. But beforehand, I'll tie you up a bit and suspend you from the ceiling. I want access to your whole body," he informed her and she quivered, with anticipation.

"You can lower your arms for now, girl," he instructed her and she obeyed immediately.

"Thank you Sir."

He returned to the cabinet and grabbed some jute rope. Unlike the one he had used the other night, this one wasn't soft. It was harsh, but he wanted to put her to the test, to see how much she was able to take on at this early stage.

He started by braiding her hair and getting it out of his way. Then he wrapped her in a tight chest harness, going down to her legs and tying them with some futomomo knots, where he tied her legs joining her ankles to her back thighs.

When he was done, he suspended her a few feet from the floor, hanging her from her harness and her legs, leaving her exposed to him, her legs wide open for him.

"I'm going to clamp your nipples, as well. It will hurt just a bit, but I'm sure you can take it," he announced, picking some adjustable nipple clamps from the cabinet.

"Yes, Sir. I'm sure you have enough personal experience to make statements on that, Sir," she replied, her eyes blazing angrily.

He chuckled, and twisted her nipples harder than necessary to get them hard and ready to clamp, and proceeded to apply the first clamp, adjusting it tightly.

She moaned in pain, biting her lips. But he didn't stop. He repeated the process with the other nipple, and when he was done, he leaned over her and licked the swollen tips.

Straightening back up, he ran a finger through her slit, confirming just how wet she was already.

"Remember, you can use your safe word any time you want. This is not a proof of endurance you have to pass, no matter what. I want to know your limits, not make you go over them," he told her, his hand grabbing her chin, making her face him.

"Yes, Sir."

"Let's start then."

He picked up the flogger and started again to run it over her skin, letting her know its softness before knowing its roughness.

The first blows were just teasers, and she enjoyed feeling them all over her skin, her legs, her belly, her back, her buttocks and even her drenched pussy. But he gradually increased the strength of the strikes and she soon was feeling the sting of each blow, and she would swear she could feel the sting of each and every string as it hit her skin, especially when he hit her breasts, making her feel more intensely the bite of the clamps attached to her nipples.

He never reached a point where the pain was unbearable. He kept it at a teasing level, even an arousing level, she had to admit.

Her body was proof of that. Her heart pounded hard in her chest, her breathing was labored and her entire body had been transformed into a huge sensor that magnified every single touch and overloaded her brain with feelings and emotions.

Alec looked at Katherine, her head thrown back, her eyes closed, the expression on her face, pure poetry. Every strike of the flogger ripped heartfelt moans from her lips, but not moans of pain or discomfort, moans of the purest pleasure.

Imprisoned in his pants, his cock was harder than ever, his craving need was reaching levels he hadn't reached in a long, long time, and now all he wanted was to take her, to make her his.

He dropped the flogger to the floor, and went closer to her, cupping her big, round breasts, in his hands, taking their clamped tips into his mouth, sucking them hard, thrilling at her whimpers and soft cries.

He unzipped his pants, released his cock and took it to the shelter of her warm lips, running it up and down a few times, smearing it in her creamy essence before he shoved it deep inside her, his hands grabbing her hips.

She let out a small cry as she felt his invasion, her walls stretching harshly to make way for him. Her whole body shuddered and her moans became louder with each deep thrust.

"Oh god, please... please... please, Sir!" her last words were loud cries and she knew that even if he didn't let her come, there was no power on earth that would make her hold back the huge orgasm building inside her.

"Come for me, girl, I want to feel the shudders of your body, clasped around me," he said, his breath showing her he was close as well.

She let go, she crossed over the edge feeling her body convulse wildly under the strength of the waves of pleasure washing over her. When her body was coming down from the heights, she felt him engorge and explode deep within her, while he lowered his head and grabbed one of her nipples between his lips, pulling hard on the clamp.

The shot of intense pain rushed through her whole body, and, once more, she was thrown back into the wildness of another orgasm, sobbing loudly.

He stood there for several minutes, before he finally slid out of her.

He zipped his pants back up, and he walked away from her toward a cabinet, leaving her there.

Missing his presence, she opened her eyes to look for him, puzzled to see him there, his hands resting on the cabinet, his head leaning down.

Alec walked away from Katherine. He needed a second for himself. He couldn't remember the last time he had felt the way he just had. His orgasm had been so much more than the physical outcome of sex. His mind, body and soul had united to create something he had trouble recognizing.

Somehow, this woman was penetrating the walls he had built around himself so carefully, so many years ago, and he wasn't going to allow that. He didn't need any more problems in his life.

He straightened his body and walked back to her, his face back to his usual mask.

He proceeded to remove the clamps from her nipples, ignoring her sobs of pain, and then put her back on the floor and cut the ropes from her body.

Katherine stayed there on the floor over the shreds of rope, caressing her suddenly cold skin, yearning his arms and his warm body, unable to understand what had happened, why he had changed so drastically.

"Please get dressed. I believe we're done for tonight," he said in his hideous cold tone.

"But I thought…" she started to say.

"Don't think, I'm sure that must be too hard for you," he interrupted, insulting her. He just wanted her out of there.

Katherine looked at him, astonished. She got up on her stumbling legs and walked to where she had left her clothes.

"Yes, you're right, I'm unable to think. Otherwise, I wouldn't have wasted a second on a cold rock like you," she said, putting on her clothes quickly and storming out of the room.

She ran through the corridor and up the stairs, her eyes clouded with accumulated tears, just to find the same crowd as before. Taking a deep breath, she walked through the room, determined not to call attention to herself.

She had almost reached the stairs leading to the main room when someone held her arm.

"Hey, how are you? Remember me?" It was Hannah.

"Oh, yes, of course. I'm fine, thank you, and you?" Katherine answered, cursing her luck.

"I'm fine, too. I just wanted to apologize for the scene earlier. I should never had done it in front of you. After all, you have nothing to do with my problems with Alec," the other woman explained.

"Don't worry about that, no harm done," She soothed her, "Listen, I really have to go now. Be well." she said, just wanting to get home.

"Wait." Hannah grabbed her by her arm again. "Are you ok? Is something wrong?" she asked, noticing the recent marks on Katherine's wrists and arms.

"Everything is just great. I'm just in a bit if a hurry," Katherine explained, with a faint smile.

"These marks are too recent. You've been in a rope scene, you shouldn't leave like that, at least, not alone." the other woman insisted.

"I assure you I'm just fine, so don't you worry about me," Katherine replied, but the woman had no intention of letting it go.

"Were you with Alec? Did he hurt in any way?" she asked, looking closely at Katherine, discovering some of the flogging welts.

"No, of course not." And it was the truth, physically speaking. The excruciating pain she felt in her heart was completely her doing. "I really have to go. Take care," she added, and pulling her arm from the other woman's hand, she disappeared into the crowd.

In just a few minutes, she was on her way home in a taxi, biting hard on her lips. She wasn't going to cry yet. She wanted privacy for that.

As soon as she slammed the door behind her, she let her body slither to the floor as she finally allowed tears to roll down her cheeks and heartfelt sobs shook her body.

When the last tear had dried on her chin, and the last sob was long gone, she slowly got up and went straight to bed.

She had tried, and it hadn't worked. So she just had to move on. Mister right was out there somewhere, and she was going to find him.

Maybe she should ask Santa Claus for help, since Christmas was around the corner.

A glimpse of herself in the full-body mirror in her room, made her realize she was still wearing the damn collar.

Enraged she took it off and tossed it across the room, before jumping on the bed, and burying her head in the pillows, shutting the world away.

Alec stood a few more minutes in the room, picking up the damaged rope and tidying the room a bit. The look on her face was still haunting him, but he was determined to forget. It was better that way, for both of them.

He finally left the room and headed up to the main dungeon. He couldn't stand being alone anymore. He needed people around, he needed distractions.

When he reached the room, the first person he saw was Hannah. Actually, she looked as if she was waiting for him.

"So the almighty Master Alec managed to destroy another submissive. I never thought you would go so low," she said in a deprecating tone. "What did you do? Did you kick her out as soon as you had what you wanted? Not even taking into consideration she had just come down from an intense rope scene, probably with some flogging included?"

For once, in all the time Alec had known Hannah, he had no words to deny her accusations. He had been so deep in his own turmoil, he had forgotten all about the care he should have provided to a submissive after such an intense scene. Drops could be dangerous, he knew that, and he had failed miserably.

"Where is she?" he asked, pleading to all the gods that Hannah had been able to stop her.

"How the hell do you expect me to know? She was your responsibility, not mine," she said, in a disdainful tone.

"Did you let her leave?" he asked, getting more and more worried.

"And how was I supposed to stop her? She insisted she was fine, and let's face it, I'm a stranger to her, why would she trust me anyway?"

"Damn!" he cursed.

"Yes, damn you, Alec. Just look around you. You're hurting everybody around you," she said, in a cold tone, walking away from him.

Alec recalled the images of Katherine lying on the floor, surrounded by the shreds of rope, looking at him as if someone had just ripped her heart out of her chest.

He had to find her. He grabbed his cell phone and dialed her number, but the call went straight to voicemail, which meant she had turned it off.

He ran up to the administration office. He needed to check her forms. Maybe she had put her address on them, although that was optional information.

"Mary, can I look at a submissive's form?" he asked erupting into the room.

"Good evening, boss. Can you tell me her name? I'll look it up for you."

"It's Katherine, but I don't remember her last name. She entered as my guest last Saturday.

"Ah, that submissive. Yes, I have her forms here, Sir," Mary said, with an intrigued smile.

Alec practically ripped the forms from his assistant's hand. He quickly went through them, but to his disappointment she hadn't provided her address.

"Damn."

"Are you trying to find this woman, boss?" Mary asked, puzzled with her boss' behavior.

"Yes, Mary."

"John just told me he had put her in a taxi. Maybe he heard her giving her address to the driver." Mary suggested, eager to help.

"Thank you, Mary." He said, storming out of the door.

He found John at the door, but he hadn't heard anything.

"Do you recall the taxi she left in?"

"No, Sir, she grabbed one that had brought someone else."

Alec ran his hand through his hair, finally admitting he wasn't going to find her, at least, not that night.

"Please check the security cameras and tell me what taxi was. You'll be able to see the taxi company and the car plates. Let me know when you have it." He ordered going back to his office. He was going to wake up the private detective he used to hire to look at people's background when they applied for membership. "Jack, how are you? I need you to find someone for me." After hearing the complaints and growls from the other man he explained the situation to him, giving him all the information he had, including the one from the taxi that John had brought him meanwhile. "I need it for as soon as possible."

"I'll do my best, but you owe man, you owe me big." Jack said, his voice already with no trace of sleep.

"Thank you."

Chapter Sixteen

He got up and decided to go home. Even with Jack's help, it would take a few hours to find her, so he would better have some sleep, or he would look like a wreck in the morning.

Once home, he was too restless to go to bed. He decided to work out for a while. Maybe if his body felt tired, his mind would find it easier to shut down for a couple of hours.

He went to his gym and while he strained his body, all he could think of was of her. How was she, what was she doing?

An hour later, soaked in sweat, he went to the shower before going straight to bed and throwing himself over it, head down, his eyes closing immediately.

A sting on his back woke him up. He raised his head to find sitting next to him a dashing reddish woman, wearing black leather, and high heel boots, carrying a crop in one of her hands.

"Rise and shine, dear!"

"Who the hell are you and what are you doing in my room?" he retorted.

"Now, what manners were you taught? That's no way of treating a lady." She replied with obvious mockery. "I thought you were expecting me. I'm the Spirit of the Present."

Alec closed his eyes in disbelief. Not again that weird dream.

"I really don't have time for this bullshit again, so why don't you go fuck somebody else's sleep?" he asked, with the coldest tone he was able to produce.

The woman sighed out loud, shaking her head. "I told them you were a lost case, but did they listen to me? No, they never listen to me!" She got up, and rested the flap of the crop underneath his chin. "I'm not happy with this either, but it's my job and you won't make me look bad with my boss, so get that yummy ass of yours up." The order was more than clear on her voice, but he was in no mood to cooperate.

He pushed the crop away and let his head fall back to the mattress, closing his eyes. Another hard sting on his back made him jump out of the bed. She was hitting him with the crop.

"What a f…?

Without letting him finish his sentence, she grabbed him by his hand and they were both catapulted to his last fight with James, just a few hours ago.

"Why are we here?" he asked, his expression closed, his tone cold.

"You pushed your best friend to walk out on you. Does this really make you happy?" she scolded him, in a cold tone, similar to his.

"I didn't push him to do anything. It was his decision to renounce to his membership." He replied, stubborn. "I'm not in the obligation of putting up with his wife's tantrums."

"No, no one would expect that from you, but you could have been a bit more understanding. You could start by believing your friend knows what he's doing, and be happy for him, for having met the right woman for him." She answered him, anger showing in her expression.

"I don't trust her, and so far she hasn't made me think I'm wrong." He insisted.

"She doesn't have to prove anything to you. Just to James, and it seems she has. You're not giving James credit for his capacity of choosing."

"I just don't want him to be hurt." Alec alleged.

"You're the one hurting him." She shouted as she grabbed him once more, making them appear in James' house. He was sitting on his back porch, a beer in hand, staring at the night. His face showed so much misery, Alec got worried instantly.

"When was this? What happened? Did anything happen to Hannah or the baby?" he turned to her, towering over the woman.

She pushed him away with the tip of the crop. "Get back, or I'll make you so tiny I could easily squeeze you between my fingers."

"Don't threaten me. Just answer the damn question." But he took a step back.

"This is happening right now. The only thing bothering James is the fact he lost his best friend and not even understands why. The day he told you Hannah was having a baby, he was ready to ask you to be the godfather, the person he trusts more to be there for his child in case of need." She informed him. "Although, my opinion he's better off without you. What could you possibly offer a baby?"

"No one asked you." He retorted, looking back at James. In that moment, Hannah came out the door and he was able to see the expression on her face. There was sadness in her eyes but also rage, and he was sure he knew to whom that rage was dedicated. She walked to James and kneeled beside him, her hands resting over her thighs, her head down.

"Sir, please, come back to bed." She begged him, in a low voice. Seeing her in her submissive role was a shock to Alec. He never thought they were living it 24/7, since he had always considered her a fake.

James turned to her, lifting her chin and kissing her deeply.

"You shouldn't be here, pet. It's too cold for you." He whispered to her, resting his face against her neck.

"I miss you, Sir. Bed is colder without you." She whispered back, tears rolling down her cheeks.

"Why are you crying pet?" James asked immediately, wiping the tears from her face.

"This is all my fault Sir. The last thing I wanted was to come between you and your best friend." She said, closing her eyes, her face showing all the hurt she was feeling.

God, was she a good actress. Alec himself almost fell for it.

"Do we have to stay here and watch this? You're only reinforcing my opinion about her: she's manipulating him." He said, cold and annoyed.

"That's what you're seeing there?" she asked him clearly furious. She looked up to the sky and yelled. "Why are you making me waste my time like this?"

Alec snorted, but made no comment.

"She loves him, truly, deeply and anyone, but you, can see that. She's suffering because she knows she's the reason why you pushed James away from your life, and because she knows you mean more than a brother to James." The woman shouted at him.

Alec looked back at the scene but refused to see it.

Enraged, the woman took him to his last scene with Katherine. He was standing, away from her, facing the wall and she was still hanging from the ropes. Her face showed the mix of feelings she was experiencing, her chest was still heaving. But her eyes were locked on him. He saw himself coming back to her, taking off her clamps, ignoring her pain, not doing a damn thing to appease it.

He had screwed that scene. He had failed her terribly.

"Why are you showing me this?" he asked her, uncomfortable.

"You're treating all women you meet as if they were clones of Rose. You don't even give them a chance. You just assume the worst and sit back waiting to turn the smallest incident into a confirmation of your assumptions."

"That's not true…"

"Yes it is, and despite all we have shown you, you still refuse to open your heart and mind to the truth. You're determined to stay on the road you drew for yourself the day your mother left your father, because she only left your father. You were the one that left her." She ranted, outraged.

Alec turned his face away from her and his eyes fell again to the scene going on down at the dungeon. He was cutting the ropes in a distant way, his hands barely touching her skin, as if he couldn't stand to touch her.

But the worst was his dismissal. He had been cruel and insulting in an unforgivable way. He was able to see the pain in her eyes, as she walked out with shaky legs.

The woman touched his hand and he was taking to a place he didn't know. When he saw Katherine, he realized it should be her place. She had let her body slide down against the door and her whole body shuddered with the violence of her sobs.

"Katherine…"

"She can't see you. Those are the consequences of your actions. You hurt all the people brave enough to get close to you."

"Stop this. This is just a mad nightmare."

"Sure, keep thinking that way and you will see how you'll end up."

She took him back to his bed and gave him a last warning.

"The Spirit of the Future will come by soon. Don't blow this chance."

Alec opened his eyes startled. He was in his bed, and his cell phone was ringing.

He reached for it and looked at the name of the person calling. It was Jack.

"I think I found her." He said as soon as he accepted the call.

"You think?" Alec asked jumping out of bed. The sun was already high in the sky.

"Well, you didn't give much to work with. Write down the address. I'm parked outside the house."

"Stay there until I arrive."

"Yes, Sir, no problem, Sir." Jack mocked him.

Alec put on some jeans and a sweater hurriedly, noticing a sting on his back, but not paying much attention to it. Right now, his priority was to find Katherine, to make sure she was alright and try to fix things between them.

Grabbing his car keys, he left immediately. He was almost there when he received a message from Jack.

"*Is this the woman*?" the question was accompanied with a picture of Katherine leaving a small house.

He sighed with relief and texted back. "*Yes, don't let her escape.*"

Chapter Seventeen

Katherine woke up in the morning feeling her whole body aching. But she knew that more than a physical ache, it was an emotional one. She felt so down, almost mournful. But she wasn't going to allow that episode to ruin her life. So he was great in bed and he had made her feel like no one else in her life ever had, that didn't change the fact that he was a badass jerk, and she was better off without him.

She was going to return to her normal life and forget that episode from her life as if it was just a simple nightmare.

She lingered in bed until noon, and then she decided to go for a walk in the park. The sun was shining and the cold air might be the right medicine for her. As she lived in the outskirts of town, her house was near a rural area, with a huge park, where you could wander for hours without seeing another soul, and that was one of the things she liked about it.

She put on some warm clothing because, despite the sun, winter was just around the corner. She grabbed her cell phone from her purse, to take it with her, and she realized it was off, so she connected it to the charger and left the house, without even turning it on.

She had been walking around the park for a several minutes, enjoying the cold breeze that ran through the fir trees' green branches, when she heard steps behind her. She stepped aside to give way to whoever it was, but the person stopped in front of her.

"Katherine."

One single word and she almost crumbled to the ground.

He was there, standing in front of her.

Alec felt a wave of relief run through his body when he saw her alright, but soon relief was replaced by rage, and all he had planned to tell her, flew out of his mind. She was his, and it was time to let her know exactly that.

"What the hell are you doing here? How did you find me?" she asked him furiously.

"It wasn't easy, believe me. Why aren't you answering your calls?" he answered, in a cold tone as usual.

"My phone is dead, and I believe it's none of your business," she replied, walking around him.

He grabbed her by her elbow and pulled her back.

"Did we end our agreement at some point and I'm not aware of it?" he asked, and she could almost feel the sharpness of the ice droplets he was throwing at her with each word.

"How can you ask that after the way you treated me last night?" she yelled at him, completely outraged by his gall.

"How did I treat you, Katherine? As MY fuck toy? Haven't you realized that's what you are? MY toy, MY slave. For me to use as I see fit?" he said, pulling her closer, his head almost touching hers, his eyes locked on hers.

"You're out of your mind if you think I would ever accept that," she shouted, struggling to free herself.

"You already did, the very instant you gave yourself to me, even if your mind still fights against it." His words sounded so fatidic, she shuddered violently.

"No, I'm not letting you do that to me," she yelled, and with a violent tug, she freed herself pushing him hard, catching him off-guard, and making him fall to the ground.

Once free, she started running with all her strength, leaving the trail, and entering the woods, needing get far away from him, but especially from his words. She didn't believe him, she couldn't.

Only moments later, she was able to hear him running after her, so she hastened her pace. She couldn't let him catch her. Deep inside her, she knew that if he took her under his spell again she would never be able to free herself from it.

But it did not take long for him to catch her. In just a few minutes, she fell as he threw himself over her, knocking her to the ground with him on top of her, crushing her against the hard ground, in a small clearing of the forest.

She struggled to kick him off of her, to no avail. He was too big for her, his body had her completely pinned to the ground and she could barely move.

"There's no escaping from me, girl, as there no escaping from yourself," he said, harshly in her ear.

"No, let me go, I don't want this anymore," she yelled, increasing her struggle, drawing strength from despair, because he was right, she was running away from herself, from the power he had over her, power she had willingly given him.

"You're mine, Katherine, and it's time for you to accept that fact," he said as he pulled her hands over her head, pinning them on the ground, with just one of his hands, while the other one pushed her pants down her legs along with her panties.

Guessing his intentions she struggled harder, to no avail. Soon his hand was slipping between her legs, reaching her pussy and rubbing her clit roughly. To her dismay, her body reacted as he knew it would, and in just seconds, she was dripping and her body was shuddering in need.

"No… stop it, don't do this!" she cried, never stopping her struggle, hearing as he unzipped his pants only seconds before he shoved his hard cock inside her.

Her cry was a tangle of emotions when she felt him inside her, pleasure fighting with pain for leadership.

"Yes, because you're mine, completely mine," he said, grunting as he plunged deep, in and out of her, his hard cock stretching her walls, assailing all in its way, marking her as his, dragging her into the spiral of the intoxicating pleasure they created every time they were together. "Say you're mine, Katherine," he demanded, never slowing his pace, "Say it!"

She sobbed, but refused to obey, still reluctant to accept that.

He released her hands, and moved his to underneath her, finding her nipples through her clothes and pinching them hard, matching the pinches with the thrusts.

"Say you're mine, girl," he repeated, pinching harder and going deeper inside her.

Her body convulsed under the strength of the wave of pleasure washing over her when she cried out:

"Yes, yes, I'm yours," she finally admitted, completely surrendering to him.

Her words were all he needed to finally let go and allow the orgasm building inside him to take over his body, making him pour himself deep inside her.

They stayed like that for a few minutes, their bodies slowly recovering from their powerful orgasms, until he slowly slid out of her, zipped his pants, and pulled up her pants, before sitting up against the trunk of a tree and pulling her into his arms, leaning her head against his chest. She had her eyes closed and he could see the tears running down her cheeks, but he knew she wasn't crying in pain. Her tears were just the way her body was releasing all the stress she had felt since he had acted like a real brute.

He caressed her hair and deposited soft kisses over it, patiently waiting for her to recover. He didn't fool himself into believing all would be roses from now on. His little shrew would fight all the way, she would probably demand more than he was willing to give, and deep down he knew he should have left her alone, that he would probably end up hurting her even more, but his selfishness didn't let him act the way he should. He wanted her too much and this time he would take what he wanted.

Katherine let him hold her in his arms, relishing his sweet caresses. Once more, she had fallen under his spell. But he was right, how was she supposed to escape her own feelings, her own needs? She knew she was going to end up burned, hurting like hell, but if she was sure of one thing, it was that meanwhile, she would live to the limit, experiencing the highest expression of pleasure and bliss.

Slowly, she opened her eyes and looked up at him, just to meet his eyes.

"Hi," he whispered.

"Hi," she whispered back, with a faint smile.

"Ready to go back home, girl?" he asked, and his tone said more than his words.

"Yes, Sir!" she accepted, meekly.

He helped her up, and got up himself.

"It came to my mind that I don't know much about your life, girl," he said as they walked back to the entrance of the park. "I had to go to a lot of trouble just to get your address."

"Oh, dear, I'm so sorry to hear that, Sir," she said, sarcasm oozing out of every single word.

He pinched her side, making her whimper.

"Sarcasm isn't allowed, girl," he said, but she could tell he didn't really mean it. "I want to know more."

"Then ask, Sir, I'll be happy to answer all your questions," she replied with a faint smile.

"What do you do for a living?" he asked, immediately.

She laughed and shook her head.

"You won't believe it, Sir," she said, amused.

"The only thing that could really shock me would be to hear you're a nun," he answered, smiling.

"No, I'm not a nun, Sir. I'm an illustrator for children's books," she said. "I basically spend the day drawing princesses and dragons," she explained, chuckling.

"Ok, I must admit I didn't see that coming," he said, laughing. "So you work from home?"

"Yes, Sir, I only have to visit the editor to deliver my job or to discuss a new one with the writer," she agreed.

"That's good. So you can work anywhere," he concluded.

"Not anywhere, Sir, I need good lighting and my drawing table. Otherwise, I can't work properly," she corrected him.

"So, if I provided you with that, would you consider moving in with me? I want to see where this will take us," he suggested, in a dead serious tone.

"Do you think that would be a good idea, Sir?" she asked, not sure she was ready for a step like that. Truth was, she barely knew him.

"I'm a Master, girl. I need to live it 24/7. I need to control every aspect of your life. I need you to hand me that control," he said, stopping and making her look at him.

"Will you share more of your life with me… Sir? she asked.

"I can promise I'll try," he said, holding her hands. "I'll respect your work, your private space. I just want to know you'll be there whenever I need you," he added.

Katherine looked at him and knowing she already was in this up to her neck, she decided, why not a bit further? She knew there was no turning back for her.

"Yes, Sir, I believe we can try," she accepted, with a smile.

He cradled her face with both his hands and kissed her passionately, and she responded with a passion that matched his perfectly.

She took him to her place and showed him her house and her work, and he only asked her for a couple of days to organize a studio for her in his house.

"I'll send for you when I get everything ready," he said when he decided to leave.

"I won't see you before that, Sir?" she asked, curious.

"No, I believe it's better this way. You can use the time to thoroughly think things through. I don't want you to feel at some level that I'm forcing you," he said, and his tone indicated he had made a decision and she wasn't going to make him change his mind.

"Alright, Sir," she accepted, not very happily. She didn't need time to think things through, but there wasn't much she could do.

"Where's your collar, girl?" he asked all of a sudden, and her face went redder than a strawberry.

"My collar... Sir? I must have put it somewhere..." she stammered, remembering how she had tossed it to the floor. She wasn't even sure where it might have landed.

"Remember, I once told you I could read you clearly?" he said, his tone cold once more.

"Yes, Sir," she sighed. "I tossed it somewhere, here in the living room, but I don't know where it fell. I was furious and hurt, Sir."

"Well, then find it. I want to see you wearing it when you enter my house in a couple of days," he ordered her.

"Yes, Sir" she answered, with a grimace.

He kissed her roughly, stealing her breath away, just before he walked to the door and left.

Chapter Eighteen

Katherine sighed, rubbing her face. She had fallen into his web once more. And the worst part was she had no intention of leaving it.

Sighing, she remembered she had to check her cell phone. Surely, she would have quite a few missed calls, and some of them certainly would be from her mother. She always called on Sundays.

She had more lost calls than she had ever had in her life. Most were from him, but she had ten calls from Lucy and 3 from her mother.

She decided to call her mom first, otherwise she would be freaking out with worry.

"Hi, Mom."

"Katherine O'Hara, where the hell have you been? I've called you a thousand times so far," she yelled at her, scolding her.

"Mom, you only called three times," Katherine said, sighing. She loved her mother, but she could be a real charmer when she wanted to be.

"On your cell, maybe, but I also called you at the house."

"I went out for a walk at the park. How's everything? Dad?"

"Don't you change the subject on me. But we are all fine. Will you come home for Thanksgiving?" she asked, getting to the point of interest for her.

"I don't think so, Mom. But I'll come for Christmas, for sure," she informed her mother.

"That's almost two months from now," her mother protested.

"I know, but right now, I don't have the time, Mom. I'll be home for a week, at Christmas. You'll grow tired of seeing me," she said, trying to appease her mother. Thanksgiving was only two weeks away, and she was sure Alec wouldn't like it if she had to leave for a whole weekend, and she did have a lot of work to deliver by the end of the month.

"I never grow tired of seeing my children," her mother protested, "I guess I'll have to wait until then."

"I knew you would understand." She chatted for a bit longer about the rest of the family before she said goodbye.

As soon as she ended the call, her phone started to buzz. It was Lucy.

"Hi, Lucy."

"Where the hell have you been? I've been trying to reach you for ages," she yelled at her, obviously concerned.

"I'm sorry I just arrived home too tired yesterday and didn't notice my cell phone was off." She explained.

"Yesterday? I thought you weren't going out yesterday."

"Yes, but something came up. I need to talk to you. Do you think you can come over for dinner, tonight or tomorrow?" she wanted another point of view on this situation, and Lucy was the only person she could trust.

"I already accepted an invitation to go out with James tonight, but I'll come tomorrow. I know you're up to something," she said, scolding her.

"I'll tell you everything, I promise." A censored version of everything, of course.

Katherine spent the rest of the day trying to get some work done, but it was hard to concentrate. She still didn't understand why he had come looking for her. After that night she would have sworn he wanted nothing else to do with her, and that had her confused. Either way, he had her hooked, to the powerful connection that existed between them, and she was going nowhere. She was his. And even while that worried her a bit, she intended to take it all the way to the end.

She prepared lasagna, Lucy's favorite, for Monday's supper, and her friend arrived with a bottle of red wine, to have with dinner.

"So, what's going on?" Lucy asked, looking at her, intensely.

Katherine sighed before she answered, pouring more wine for both of them.

"Do you remember the other night when I went clubbing alone?" she started, and she told her all she thought Lucy should know, a much-censored version of all the facts.

"And now you're moving in with this guy?" Lucy practically yelled at her.

"Yes, I've made up my mind."

"Katherine, of all the crazy things you have done in your life, this must be the worst," she scolded her, "You practically know nothing about this guy; he could be a serial killer."

"Come on, Lucy, don't overreact. This will be the best way for me to get to know him. Lucy, he makes me feel like nobody else. I have no words to describe it," she explained. She needed Lucy's support on this adventure.

"I want to meet him. You sound obfuscated by him, and I need to be sure he won't harm you."

"He won't, but I'll set up a meeting between you two, ok?"

"Good. But please be careful, and always keep your damned cell phone on."

"I will, I promise."

Chapter Nineteen

Alec arrived on Tuesday morning with a huge pickup truck. She had packed a few boxes with her working materials, clothes and other personal items she might need, so it was thoughtful of him to come in that vehicle.

He hopped out of it and strode towards her, claiming a hard kiss from her that told her just how much he had missed her.

"Are you ready?" he asked her, his face plain, with no expression on it.

"Yes, I have a few boxes in the hall. I just realized I don't even know where you live," she told him, showing him the way.

He mentioned one of the most expensive condos in town, and she gasped, surprised. She knew he had money, she just hadn't imagined it was that much.

"My house is big, so you'll have plenty of space for you and your work," he added.

"Nice." What else could she say? "Let's take these boxes to your pickup truck then." She suggested, but he was looking at her with a deep frown. "What's the matter?"

"You're not wearing your collar. And you haven't addressed me correctly ever since I got here," his tone was cold, and his expression promised nothing more than problems for her.

"I thought we were starting it when we got to your place... Sir," she answered, hugging herself.

"I told you we never stopped, girl," his tone got even colder.

"Well, I didn't understand it that way. Maybe next time you can be clearer... Sir." She said, resting her hands over her hips in a very defiant manner.

His face twisted into a very devious grin, and he slowly walk towards her.

Katherine took a look at his face and decided her best option was to run, and she did. She turned away and ran as fast as she could to her bedroom, and turned to lock the door on him, but she wasn't fast enough.

He pushed the door open almost effortlessly, and then locked it behind him. She ran and put the bed between them.

"So, girl, you think I should be clearer?" he asked in a sarcastic tone.

Katherine knew she was lost, so she threw caution to hell.

"Yes, that would be very helpful... Sir." The pause before the word 'sir' was on purpose, and long enough for it to be impossible not to notice.

His grin became even more devious.

"Well, girl, let me be clear with you. My orders are to be followed, no questions asked, immediately. Otherwise, there will be consequences, and depending on the fault those consequences will vary in intensity, strength and length." His words were clear and precise without leaving anything to doubt. "While we are alone, at the house, the club or wherever I see fit, you'll wear your collar. You'll always, ALWAYS, address me with respect. You can use the word 'Sir' if we are in public, but from now on, you'll use 'Master', all the time in private," he added, walking slowly towards her, on the other side of the bed.

"Now, see? That's a clear message... Master." Again, she defied him, even knowing there was no escape for her. But for some reason, she needed to poke him, she needed to see how far she could push him.

"I'm glad you find it so, girl, that means you know what comes next." He closed the distance between them with two strides, but she jumped over the bed to escape him. Once more, he was faster than her, and in a split second, he had her pinned against the mattress, face down, one hand at her nape, and a knee over her legs. With his free hand, he lowered her pants along with her panties, exposing her buttocks. "Now, let me show you one of the consequences of disobeying me," he said, just before his hand fell hard over her right cheek.

She let out a small cry, as the shot of pain ran through her body. She didn't have much time to recover from it before the next blows hit her, making her whimper. With tears rolling down her cheeks, she lost count of the blows, since he dropped them in a fast succession, of sharp, painful smacks that set her buttocks on fire.

"Did you get this message clearly, girl?" he asked her when he was done, running his hand gently over the abused skin.

"Yes, Master," the answer came between sobs, her body still over the bed. She could feel the sting from the blows, but oddly, she didn't feel hurt, the emotion rushing wildly through her was relief, and that warm feeling you get when you arrive home after a long absence. Things were back as they were supposed to be.

"Good girl." He lowered his head and deposited a million little kisses all over her buttocks, his hand still caressing her, his fingers sliding down to her slit, finding, with delight, her pussy completely drenched and palpitating with untamed need.

He quickly unzipped his pants, releasing his throbbing cock, and pulled her to her all fours before he plunged it deep inside her.

Her moan of pure ecstasy, as he entered her, was music to his ears and he pounded in and out of her, fast and deep until he drove them both into the arms of a powerful orgasm.

He hopped out of bed a few minutes later, zipping his pants back up and helping her to do the same with hers.

"From now on, you'll only wear pants when I tell you to. Otherwise, they are strictly forbidden," he announced as he finished helping her.

"May I ask you why, Master?" In her voice still lingered the effects of what had just happened between them.

"Yes, you may. Pants don't give me a quick access to you, girl. They are quite a nuisance." He accompanied his answer with a naughty wink that made her giggle. "Now, please get your collar. I want you to have it on when you get to your new home."

"Yes, Sir." She picked it up from her purse, and brought it to him, getting on her knees before offering it to him.

She wasn't able to see his expression when she did it, or she would have been extremely happy. Her natural act of getting on her knees before him had touched a cord inside him he believed to be dead.

He wrapped the collar around her neck and helped her up.

Between the two of them, they loaded the pickup, and she checked the house, making sure everything was locked.

"I'll follow you in my car, Master," she informed him as they were getting ready to leave.

"You have a car?" he asked, surprised since he hadn't seen her with it.

"Yes, Master, it's that one. I normally don't use it when I go out at night." She pointed at a small, old car parked just in front of the small house.

"You don't need to take your car, you can use one of mine, if you need it." His expression told her he didn't like the fact she owned a car, and that puzzled her.

"I'm afraid I can't leave it here, Master. Though this is a very quiet area, a car parked in the street for too long attracts petty thieves," she explained, patiently, rolling her eyes.

His hand flew to her chin, making her face him.

"Wait, Master, I know!" she said before he could open his mouth. "No rolling eyes at you, right?"

Alec looked at her deliberating whether to smack her or kiss her. "You're a smartass, aren't you girl?"

"I believe you had established that prior to today, Master," she answered with a broad smile. She was determined to melt the ice around this man. Even if it meant her ass would never be white again.

He chuckled and nibbled her lips hard. "Don't lose me in the traffic," he said, closing the subject.

"I wouldn't dare, Master."

They arrived at his place almost an hour later. Like she had imagined when he mentioned where he lived, his house was really a mansion. Of modern design, with huge windows from floor to ceiling, with two floors, it looked awesome. Around it he had huge gardens with grass, bushes and trees.

She parked behind his pickup and hopped out of her car, meeting him at the entrance.

"So, what do you think of it, girl?" he asked.

"It looks beautiful, Master. I'm sure I'll love to live here."

Once inside, he took her to her own room, decorated in tons of soft peach, with a fantastic canopy bed. "I sleep alone. I've always slept alone and I'm not changing that." That was his explanation to her silent question, and although she found the idea abhorrent, she didn't make any comment.

The room he had chosen for her studio was just perfect, with the perfect lighting and the best drawing table she could ask for. She started unpacking her things immediately and in less than an hour she was settled in, and she went to meet him in the living room. He had offered her his help but she had declined politely, she needed to organize her own things or she would never find anything.

"Have you finished, girl?" he patted the couch near him, inviting her to sit next to him.

"Yes, Master, it's all done." She sat with a sigh, sitting next to him. "I would like to ask you something, Master."

"Always feel free to ask whatever you want, unless I've instructed you to be silent, of course."

"Of course, Master." The grin on her face was of pure amusement. "I would like you to establish clearly the rules, now that we'll be living together. What do you expect from me? What will be my duties here, Master?"

"Your duties here will be to obey any order that I might give you. I have a housekeeper, a cook, a gardener and a chauffeur, so you don't need to worry about the housework, nor cooking unless you want to. As for the rules, you already have the basics. I don't expect you to wait for me at the door, because I know you work at home, but I do expect you to drop work and greet me when I enter your studio, after a long absence."

"Can you please define long, Master?"

"Of more than 5 hours, for example."

"And how am I to greet you, Master?"

"By coming to meet me and assuming your waiting position, girl. The other rules will be established along the way," he answered, losing his patience. "You ask too much, girl."

"I'm just trying to keep my ass in good health, Master," she replied with a grimace.

He chuckled and pulled her towards his chest, making her rest her head over him. "I'll never be bored around you, right?"

"I truly hope not, Master."

"We will dedicate a couple of weeks to testing your limits regarding the things I love in this lifestyle, and introducing you to them, since you barely have any experience in it." His fingers ran through her hair, gently.

"Are we going to visit the club a lot then, Master?" she asked, curious.

"No, I have a small dungeon here at the house, with the basics, but once in a while we will visit the club. I need to be there at least on Fridays and Saturdays."

"Why is that, Master?"

"Because I own it." His answer surprised her a lot, but it explained a lot of things.

"That's what you do for a living, Master?" A fast smack landed on her sore buttocks acknowledging her slip of the tongue.

"No, I have a construction company as well, girl. Now, let's grab some dinner. Tonight I want to get to bed early."

And so things slowly entered into some sort of routine. Every night, after dinner he would take her to his so-called small dungeon, that had nothing to envy about the ones at the club, and he would patiently introduce her to his favorite devices and instruments. Eager to learn all she could, she gave him little reason for him to punish her, but even so, once in a while her tongue gave her a hard time.

He had been right about her, and she could accept now the truth that she thrilled on pain, when applied to enhance pleasure. She still dreaded his punishments, or so she kept telling herself, but when his purpose was to create the most amazing orgasms she had experienced in her life, that was a whole different story.

Chapter Twenty

They went back to the club that first Friday. Besides going to check on things at the club, he wanted her to watch another performance with the needle expert. He was eager for her to let him try that on her, but she had been too afraid and he still hadn't forced her to face that fear in particular.

After all, he had rendered her doubts regarding anal sex meaningless, and now she was being trained for it. He had her wearing a butt plug several hours a day, and though she was still furious with him, she was thankful. He was way too big for a virgin ass like hers.

At the club, he sat at a table and he had her kneel next to him on a cushion on the floor. Several people came to greet him, and he had introduced her to most of them.

She was sad to realize he didn't have close friends in that crowd. They all knew him and respected him, but he kept them all at a safe distance, until James showed up. She noticed he became tense the minute James appeared.

He sat at the table and look at Alec and then at Katherine.

"You already collared her?" his questions made Alec pucker his lips, with disgruntlement.

"I don't believe that's any of your business," Alec answered through gritted teeth.

"And yet, you feel you have the right to judge my relationship with Hannah."

"You barely knew her when she managed to drag you down the aisle."

"Alec, she didn't drag me anywhere. The day she agreed to be mine, my wife, my submissive, was the happiest day of my life, up until then. She means the world to me and I just wish you could meet someone and experience a tenth of the feelings I share with Hannah." James replied, with passion in his voice.

"You're just fooling yourself, and one day you'll realize that." Alec's answer was cold and distant.

James shook his head, giving up. He looked at Katherine instead. "Don't let him steal your heart, he will crush into thin dust." He got up and left.

Katherine stayed in silence, knowing it was too late for that warning and feeling the waves of tension emanating from Alec.

Suddenly, he got up and gestured her to do the same. "Let's go visit Lady Deviant. She should be ready for her performance." His tone was colder than ever, and his face only showed tension.

She followed him, a bit worried, but trying not to pay much attention to the whole thing. She knew what she was getting into and that she would pay the price, so she just had to face it and live it up to the limits until then.

They reached a small stage and the woman was getting ready to show her art with the needles.

They took a seat at a nearby table, and this time he made her sit on his lap, his hands clasped around her waist.

This time, Lady Deviant was using small needles, the ones used on syringes, and she had in her tray at least three different sizes, judging by the colors. She started with the smallest ones, piercing her submissive's breast, drawing a circle around the nipple with them. She picked the next size, larger than the first and drew a circle around the first one, before using the third group of needles, repeating the process. The final result was beautiful. Three rows of colorful needles piercing both breasts.

During the whole performance, Katherine's attention had been focused on the submissive and her reactions to the needles, because she knew Alec was going to ask her to experience it, since it was one of his favorite fetishes. Even so, she was aware of Alec's body, feeling how the tension he had experienced was slowly going away, and he relaxed, watching the show.

The submissive obviously felt pain, but it was also obvious that the pain was an instrument of her pleasure. The bliss written on her face was so clear, you could almost envy its deepness.

Lady Deviant exposed the submissive's pussy to the audience, just to show how aroused the woman was. She then grabbed a Hitachi wand and pressed it to the throbbing clitoris and it only took her seconds to come wildly.

Lady Deviant claimed her mouth in a passionate kiss before she proceeded to remove the needles.

Katherine was concentrating on looking at the scene when she felt Alec's hand sliding underneath her skirt and panties, chuckling when he discovered her drenched pussy.

"Did you like what you saw, girl?" he whispered in her ear, kissing and nibbling it.

"I'm invoking the Fifth Amendment, Master, there's no way I'm answering that question," she answered, avoiding his eyes, struggling to ignore his fingers running around her pussy.

"I'm afraid that doesn't work with me, girl. I own you, I own that precious body of yours, your mind, even your soul." His answered was accompanied with a very arrogant smile.

"Oh, Master, don't you think that's being a bit greedy? My soul belongs to God and no one else," she replied, obviously teasing him.

In response to her words, his fingers found her clit and pinched it hard, ripping a loud moan from her lips.

"Answer my question, girl." The order was unmistakable, and she felt compelled to answer.

"Yes, Master, for some weird reason I find that extremely arousing. But I'm not sure I could go through with it." Her answer was honest and showed her doubts about something so extreme, that she had never even considered trying it, until she met him.

"I understand that, and I'm just asking you to try. We'll go slowly, a step at a time. Do you think you can do that?" his eyes were locked on hers and his fingers never left her pussy.

Katherine moaned and squirmed in his lap.

"Oh, that's so unfair, Master, I can't think straight like that."

He laughed rubbing his nose on her neck.

"I never said I was fair." He kissed and nibbled her earlobe. "So tell me, are you willing to try it?"

Katherine sighed, but she knew she wasn't going to say no. She really wanted to please him, and her curiosity and desire to experience it grew with every time she learned more about it.

"Yes, Master, I'm willing to try," she acquiesced.

"Do you want your first experience to be with me or would you prefer to have it at the hands of Lady Deviant? She is far more experienced than me," he said, his other hand grabbing one of her breasts.

She gave it some thought, but actually, she had no doubts. "With you, Master, I have no desire to experience anything with anyone else."

He kissed her deeply, happy with her answer, his fingers pushing her harder to the edge, rubbing, pinching her knob and her nipple.

"Master…" she begged, gasping for air, feeling the orgasm building inside her.

"Come for me, girl." He whispered in her ear, pressing harder, pushing her more and more. And she came hard, furiously, all over his fingers, not aware of anything else other than him and the pleasure he was giving her and he muffled her moans by kissing her.

When calm returned to her body, he finally took his fingers out of her, presenting them to her, coated in her juices.

"Clean them up for me," he demanded, and she looked at him and at his fingers, doubting. She had never tasted her own juices, but he wasn't giving her any choice, so she opened her mouth and let him put them inside, licking them, and tasting its bitter sweetness, until she had them cleaned.

He finally took his fingers out of her mouth and kissed her once more.

"Let's do it." He helped her up, and got up.

"What? Now... Master?" she looked at him, horrified. She wasn't ready for that.

"There's no better moment than the present, girl."

"I'm not ready, Master," she protested.

"You will never be ready, girl." She knew he was right, but even so...

He didn't let her say another word. He dragged her behind him, directly to the thematic rooms, and in no time, they were standing in front of the one labeled as Doctor's Office. He opened the door and let her in.

The place looked pretty much like a real doctor's office, with its white tiles, and its sterilized looks, an examination table, and even a gynecologist's table, with cabinets filled with medical instruments.

"You're very realistic with the decors, Master." She admired the room.

"We do our best." He guided her to the gynecologist's table and after taking all her clothes out, he helped her up. "Since this is your first time, I'm going to restrain you on the table, because I can't trust you to stay still. Keep in mind that you will always be able to call RED, if you find it more than you can take. Just don't act out of cowardice."

"I've never been a coward and I won't become one now… Master," she retorted, and he chuckled.

"Good." He made her lie on the table, set her buttocks on its edge and started to restrain her with the leather straps and the cuffs added to the table, and soon she wasn't able to move more than her fingers and her head.

He kissed her gently on her lips. "Since it's your first time, I'll use small, thin needles on you, and only four in each breast," he told her, while his hands kneaded her breasts and his fingers twisted and pinched her nipples getting them really hard.

Her breath was getting heavier and her heart was hammering hard in her chest.

"Yes, Master."

He picked up one of the needles and she closed her eyes, but a second later, she opened them again. She had to see it.

Alec smiled, approving of her courage, and teased her right nipple before he pushed the needle into her breast at the base of the nipple.

She let out a small cry when she felt it go in, the shot of pain rushing through her body. She was still panting from the first one when he inserted the second one, and the third and the fourth, forming an 'X' around the nipple.

"How are you feeling?" he asked, brushing the tip of his finger over the nipple, and she gasped for air, as swirls of pain and pleasure irradiated to all her breast.

"Don't ask me questions I can't answer, Master," She huffed between harsh intakes of air, feeling the sting of the needles each time she breathed.

"Are you giving me orders, girl?" he asked with a touch of fun.

"No, Master, I'm begging," she answered quickly. "I can't think."

He kissed her hard, his finger still playing with her nipple.

He finally let her breath and walked around the table to get to her other nipple.

Knowing what was coming, she whimpered, tiny beads of sweat appearing on her forehead. He repeated the process, and although the sting had to feel the same, somehow she felt it more. Not more pain, it was as if her body was more sensitive to everything, and sensations were multiplied a thousand times.

Shudders rippled through her body, and she sobbed.

He was done, and he took a step back to admire his work. She looked so beautiful. With her eyes closed, her lips tight, the expression on her face was beyond words. He took his cell phone out and took a few pictures of her. He was sure she would love to see them.

Laying the phone aside, he returned next to her, between her spread legs, kissing her belly gently, making her open wide her eyes.

"You look so beautiful, girl." His kisses drew a fire trail up to her aching nipples. He lingered over it with his tongue out for a few seconds, before he finally licked it, circling the nipple just above the needles, and then pressing the hard tip down, relishing on her sobs and her pleas. He slid his hand between her legs, reaching her dripping pussy and finding her engorged knob, slightly rubbing it a couple of times.

Katherine was dizzy. Feelings and emotions raged through her and she wasn't able to distinguish what she was feeling. Pain, pleasure and everything in between mingled inside her, and she felt on the verge of something she couldn't even recognize.

When she felt Alec kissing her, escalating his way up to her breasts and licking her nipple, she almost lost it. But when she felt his fingers over her aching clit, she was overtaken by a powerful orgasm, pleasure and pain ripping through her body in perfect harmony.

He didn't wait for her to come down; unzipping his pants, he released his hard cock and thrust it deep inside her, plunging it in and out hard, fast and deep, his mouth still playing with her sore nipples, dragging her along with him in the untamed waves of another orgasm.

When he was able to get air into his lungs again, he slowly pulled out of her, cleaned himself up, and zipped his pants back up.

Picking up an antiseptic solution, he withdrew the needles with quick, clean movements, and applied the solution, hearing her whimpers. As always, there was little blood, but he cleaned the area thoroughly.

He removed the restraints and carried her to a couch in one of the corners of the room and just held her there, in his arms, cuddling her.

Katherine was drained. Physically and emotionally. She hadn't expected it to be so intense, so powerful, so mind-blowing.

She just wanted to cuddle in his arms forever and close her eyes until her body and mind reached their balance again.

"Do you want to go home, girl?" he asked, whispering in her ear.

She forced her brain to work for a few seconds. Home meant going to an empty room, sleeping alone in a huge bed. No, she didn't want to go home, not yet. She needed his presence; she needed to feel him close.

"No, Master, I just need a couple more minutes. Then I'll be alright," she whispered, trying to keep him from knowing just how deep was her need for him.

"Very well, girl." And he stayed there, caressing her, cuddling her until she felt strong enough to get up.

They went back to the main room of the club and she accompanied him during his rounds through the club and during his visit to the administrator's office, Miss Mary, as he introduced her.

Dawn was making its way up in the horizon when they finally left the club to go back home. She wanted to beg him to stay with her that night, but she wasn't able to say a word. Tonight she wasn't strong enough to bear a negative, so she just walked straight to her room and dropped her exhausted body over the covers, not even bothering with going under them, her eyes closing with a sad sigh, as she surrendered to sleep.

When she opened her eyes again, she was under the covers, and she could swear the pillow next to her had been used, but she dismissed the whole idea, determined not to get her hopes up.

She got up and picked her phone. It was Sunday, so she would better call her mother before she tried to call her. She had no intention to tell her she had moved in with a man she barely knew. Her parents would never approve that.

At mid-afternoon, while she was working a little in her studio, she had a call from Lucy.

"Hi Lucy, how's everything?" she asked, pleased to hear from her friend.

"Fine, just great. What about you? How's everything going in your new house?"

"Fine, too. We're slowly getting to know each other, and building our relationship."

"*Have you told your parents about it*?" Lucy asked, her tone indicating she already knew the answer.

"No, and I won't, not yet, you know that."

"Because you know they won't like it at all."

"I know, I just need a bit more time, then I'll tell them." Or so she hoped. Telling her parents meant that they would want to meet Alec, and somehow she couldn't see him agreeing to that.

"Are you coming over to Thanksgiving, as always? That would be a good opportunity for me to meet him." Lucy asked.

"Oh, right, it's next week… I had lost track of time. I haven't talked about it with him but I will and I'll let you know." She frowned, not sure what he would think of the idea. So far, their social life had been limited to the club. He hadn't introduced her to any friends or business acquaintances outside the club.

"Nice, you know I'm counting with your pumpkin pie." Lucy remembered her.

"I know, don't worry."

She chatted a few more minutes with her before she ended the call.

Putting the cell phone back in her skirt's pocket, she decided to go looking for him.

He was watching a football game in the huge plasma TV. Unsure if to interrupt him, or not she stayed at the door, a few moments looking at him.

"Don't stand there, girl. Join me." He ordered, sensing her presence.

She walked towards him kneeling beside him on the floor. He caressed her hair, before he pulled her up to sit over his lap.

"Are you done working for today?" he asked, holding her close to him.

"Yes Master."

"Good, maybe we could go out for a walk." He suggested, rubbing his nose in her neck, inhaling her scent.

"That would be great, Master." She answered, gathering courage to ask him about Lucy's invitation. She still had trouble defining how she should or shouldn't act in moments like this one. "Can I ask you something, Master?"

"Yes, you can speak freely, unless told otherwise." He clarified.

"Thank you Master. My best friend Lucy called me. Next week is Thanks Giving, and I usually spend the night with her and her family." She explained, cautiously. "As usual, she called me to

invite me and added you to the invitation, Master."
She continued.

Underneath her she felt his body stiffen, just
before he put her on the couch and got up. He walk
to the window and looked out the window. "I don't
celebrate any holidays." He finally said, in a cold
tone, before turning to look at her. "If you want to
go and celebrate with your friends, I'll allow you to
go, but don't count with me."

"Even if you don't celebrate holidays, I believe it
would be a good time for you to meet some of my
friends, Master." She tried once more.

"There's no need for me to meet your friends."
He replied, his face turning into the usual mask.

"But, they feel the need to meet you, Master."
She got up from the couch, unable to stay still,
feeling the hard squeeze of disappointment over her
heart.

"I'm sure you'll think of something to erase that
need, since I don't have any intention of doing
that." His tone was harsh and the cold shine of his
eyes told her she wasn't going anywhere with this,
so she decided to drop it.

"As you wish, Master. Even so, I would love to
go. It's an important thing for me." She asked,
determined to not allow him to keep her apart from
her friends.

"Very well, you can go then. I'm sure you'll have a good time." He accepted, closing the distance between them, claiming a hard kiss from her lips. "Go get a warm sweater and put on some pants. It's cold outside."

"Yes, Master." She left the room to go change clothes. She wanted to argue with him about his decision, but she decided to leave that battle for when she had to convince him to meet her parents. If before she had doubts about his reaction, now she knew with would be an almost impossible battle to win.

She joined him at the hall and they went for a walk. She loved those walks, since he always gave her his arm for support and they would stroll just like any other couple.

The morning of Thanksgiving, after he left for work, Katherine dedicated some time to bake a couple of pumpkin pies; she wanted to leave him one, and the other one was for Lucy. Her friend hadn't been very happy when she told her Alec wasn't going. It made her suspicious of him, and Katherine had trouble convincing her it was alright.

Around lunch time, she was working in her studio when someone opened the door, startling her. She raised her head and looked with surprise at him standing at the door. It was the first time he came home at this hour.

She got up and walked to him, kneeling next to him, assuming the waiting position. "Hello, Master, I didn't expect you this early."

"I thought that since you'll deprive me of your presence tonight I might as well take pleasure in it this afternoon." He said, caressing her head, his tone sarcastic, letting know it didn't please him she went to the dinner.

"I'm glad, Master." She answered him, ignoring his claim. Not going to the dinner to stay with him would only make Lucy more disgruntled with the situation and she loved her friend way too much to create problems with her.

He helped her up, and without uttering another word he took her to the dungeon, on the basement.

She could sense he was in a strange mood, so she tried not to make it worst. She didn't want a fight over some stupid detail or something similar.

Once inside the dungeon, he quickly helped her out of her clothes and took her to the cross, cuffing her to it, facing the cross.

He ran his hands through her body, before he stopped behind her, and whispered in her ear. "I want to use the belt on you today. I want you to remember me tonight every time you move, every time you take a seat." There was a raw need in every one of his words. A need to mark her as his, to make sure she remembered all the time to whom she belonged to, and she understood it, and she accepted it.

"Yes Master."

He unbuckled his belt and took it off his pants, and she prepared herself for it. So far he hadn't used the belt on her, but he had used other things as hard as a belt. She knew she could use the safe word if she found it more than she could take, but so far he always seemed to know just how far he could go, and he always stopped before. She always ended up experiencing powerful orgasms after those sessions.

The first blow landed in her buttocks and she bit her lips trying to muffle the cry. It hurt, the shot of pain rushed through her body, but she could take it. She wanted to.

He continued striking her, in her buttocks, in her thighs, in her back, pushing more and more to the edge, until he dropped the belt to shove himself deep inside her, easily dragging her with him, to the orgasm he had been building inside them.

She had to change her mind about the clothes she was wearing that night. She had chosen a short, red dress, with a nice cleavage in the back, but with it anyone could see the red welts he had left on her back and on her thighs. So she chose instead a red silk blouse and black pants. She combed her hair in a loose braid that fell on her shoulder and she was ready. Looking at her reflection on the mirror, she noticed her collar. She had grown so used to it, that she had put it back on after her shower. Slowly she took it off again, leaving it over her dressing table.

She went downstairs to grab the pie and call a taxi. Alec was in the kitchen when she came in. "Oh, I left you some pumpkin pie, Master, in case you like it."

"Did you bake it?" he asked, looking at her, frowning.

"Yes, Master, sometimes I think Lucy only invites me because she wants my pie." She answered teasingly, trying to erase the frown from his face.

"Why are you wearing pants, girl?" he asked, in a cold tone.

"Ah, yes, I wasn't going to, Master, but the dress I was going to wear showed the welts on my thighs." She explained.

"I see. Where did you leave your collar?" he asked, his expression getting even darker.

"In my room. Most of the friends going to this party know nothing about my kinky side, and I want to keep it that way, Master." She explained.

"Why? Are you ashamed of it?"

"No, but there is still a lot of ignorance regarding BDSM, and most people still consider it taboo. In my line of work I need to be discreet."

"Very well. Wait here."

"Yes Master, I'll call the taxi." She said as he started to walk out the door. Her words though, made him stop.

"Taxi?"

"Yes Master, I don't like to drive when I go out at night."

"No taxis, I'll drive you, and when you're done I'll pick you up." He informed.

"That doesn't make any sense…"

"I wasn't asking you your opinion." He cut her, storming out of the kitchen.

She sighed, trying to understand the complex man her heart had chosen to love. Because she loved him, she had no doubts about it.

He returned in only a few moments. "I was saving this for our first night out together, in a public place, but I think this a better moment." He said handing her a small box. "Open it."

She took it, not sure she wanted to see it, but she slowly opened it, gasping with the surprise.

It was a collar, but this one was made of gold and platinum, a chain formed by symbols of infinity with a heart shaped pendant. But not, just any heart. This one had a lock on it. It was beautiful.

"Do you like it?" he asked her, a bit wary.

"It's gorgeous! I've never seen anything so beautiful, Master." She answered, still looking at it, feeling a tear escaping the corner of her eye.

"Will you wear it?" he asked.

"Of course I will, Master." She accepted, and kneeling she handed the collar to him.

With a grin, he took the collar from the box and wrapped it around her neck, locking it in its place.

"Now, you're ready." He said, helping her up and kissing her.

"Thank you Master."

"Let's go now, before I change my mind." He said walking to the garage.

When they arrived at Lucy's place he insisted once more for her to call him, and she accepted knowing he wasn't going to change his mind.

The party was fun and she enjoyed spending time with her friends, but he had done a good job on her and she was unable to take him out of her mind. And when she did, a rush of pain through her body from a sudden movement would take her right back at it. She missed him very much and it just wasn't the same without him beside her.

He picked her up when the party was over and that night he fucked her as if there was no tomorrow, with a hint of desperation in every touch, in every kiss.

Weeks went by in what she felt was light speed, and though she tried to talk to him about Christmas, she always ended up postponing the subject until there was no more time. They were two days away from Christmas Eve and her mother was expecting her home that night. Her parents lived five hours from her town, so she had to talk to him that morning.

She went looking for him at his study, praying to convince him to do this for her.

"Master, I need to tell you something." She entered the room, finding him seated by his desk.

"Yes, girl, what's the problem?" he frowned a bit, looking up.

"I know you don't celebrate the holidays, but I do, Master, and so does my whole family." She started, twisting her hands out of nervousness. "I know I should have told you about this earlier, but it never seemed to be the right moment..."

"Get to the point Katherine." He ordered and his frown grew deeper.

"I'm expected tonight at my parents' house to spend the next week, Master. It's tradition for us to gather the whole family for Christmas." She explained.

"I see."

"So far, I was able to keep from my parents, the fact that I moved in with you..."

Alec stiffened when he heard her. "Why did you do that? It shames you to live with me?" he interrupted her.

"Of course not, Master, but if I had told them, they would have demanded to know you, and it didn't feel the right moment for that." She tried to explain. "But I can't keep omitting it to them. So I thought this could be the perfect moment to tell them and for you to meet them."

A thick silence fell in the room. His face had turned into that hideous mask he used to wear when something disgruntled him.

Alec got up, and crossed his arms over his chest. What were her intentions? Was she trying to force him into assuming a compromise with her? Maybe he had made a huge mistake when he brought her to his house. "What makes you think I want to meet your family?" he asked in a disdainful tone.

"The fact this is very important to me, or otherwise I wouldn't be asking you, Master." She said, starting to feel the squeeze of an iron fist over her heart. She had known this wasn't going to be easy. "My parents would be extremely worried if I told them I had moved in with a man that doesn't want to meet them."

"Then don't tell them." He retorted.

"I can't do that anymore, Master. You don't have to spend the whole week there, you just need to show up and let them know you."

"No." His answer was curt and emotionless.

"Why not, Master? Am I asking that much?" she insisted, feeling the grip in her heart tightening.

"Because it's pointless. It's not like I'm your boyfriend or something similar. I've never met any family member of my previous slaves and I see no reason to start with you. What we have between us, has nothing to do with them, the same way it has nothing to do with your friends or mine for that matter." He explained, trying to convince himself of his own words.

"What do we have between us, then? What am I to you?" she asked, stiffening, having trouble to accept what she was hearing.

His face became as impassive as a rock. "I thought I had let that clear when I asked you to move in with me, Katherine." He said, impatiently scolding her. "You're just my last fuck toy, a good fuck toy, but still a toy." He answered, his eyes locked on hers, to make sure she had no doubt about it, even when every word tasted like lies in his mouth.

She looked at him in total disbelief. She couldn't believe he was actually saying that.

"Why did you go through all the trouble of looking for me?" she asked, struggling to utter every word.

"You had proven to be a good fuck toy." He insisted.

"Stop calling me that." She yelled, overwhelmed by the pain crushing her heart. "I'm no toy, I'm a person, and one with feelings, but I'm sure you have no idea what that means. A damn rock has more feelings than you."

"You can't say I didn't tell you from the beginning what I wanted from you, so this argument has no sense. You're free to do whatever you want with your parents, but be certain I'll never accept to meet them." He said, colder than ever, dismissing the whole subject.

"Don't worry; I would never expose them to a pitiful excuse of a human being like you." She retorted.

"Sadly, you're right, I can't say I wasn't warned. This time, stay out of my life. I'm sure you'll find a replacement for me in a blink of an eye."

"Are you going to make this a habit? To storm out every time things don't work the way you would want them to?" the annoyance in his voice was remarkable.

"Do you think I could stay after the things you just said?" her astonishment was big.

"I fail to see the novelty of what I said. The day I asked you to move in with me I told you what I wanted from you, I told you, you were my toy, my slave. So what changed?"

"Silly of me, I never thought you meant it. So you can say that I changed." She replied.

"No, you didn't. You just think you did. I can still make you feel like no one else can." He assured her.

"You are probably right, but it's not enough for me. I want more, I deserve more, and you obviously aren't going to give me more."

"I'm giving you all I can." Somehow those words sounded familiar to his hears, but he refused to analyze it. He wasn't going to change, he didn't want to.

"Well, I'm afraid that's not enough for me. I'll send someone to pick up my things." With tears gathering in her eyes, she left the room and walked to the bedroom she had been using and that had never felt like it was hers.

She gathered the bag she had prepared for the trip to her parent's house and taking her collar out and leaving in over the bed, she left the house, got in her car and left the place without looking back.

A few miles later she had to stop the car. Tears rolling down her cheeks made it impossible for her to see. She let tears fall and cried out all the pain she felt inside her. When she finally calmed down, she started the car and drove off to her parents' house.

Chapter Twenty Three

In his study, Alec stared at the door, for a few moments feeling a strange sensation on his chest. She was leaving him, again. Well, surely it was the best. She was starting to demand more than he was willing to give.

He poured a scotch and drank it of a single sip, pouring another one right away. He walked to the widow and looked out, just in time to see her car disappear into the street. He closed his eyes for a second, forcing himself to believe this was for the best. He sipped the drink he was holding in his hand, feeling the burning from the scotch down his throat.

He had to keep busy. So he decided to go to work and forget all about it. After all she was right, he would find another submissive in a split second.

He returned to the house late at night, still feeling like shit. He had been drinking the whole day, and not even alcohol had given him the numbness he was looking for. The weight in his chest didn't go away, by the contrary, it only grew heavier and heavier as the day went by.

The moment he entered the house, a deep silence was the only thing that greeted him, so he went straight to his study, decided to keep drinking. He wanted to forget. Just for today. He hadn't been able to take her words out of his mind, playing them in his head over and over.

With the bottle in his hand he threw himself over the chaise longue near the window and, just drank himself to sleep.

Alec felt a kick in his hip and the next thing he knew he was landing on the floor, tripping with the empty bottle of scotch.

"What the fuck...?"

"Are you planning on sleeping while your life goes down the drain?" a male voice sounded from behind him.

Still on the floor, feeling a thousand stabs in his head, Alec turned to see who was there. A man, around his age, dressed in black leather, heavy boots and holding a leather paddle in his hands.

"Who the hell are you?" he muttered, slowly getting up.

"I would say that by now you should know the answer to that. Is your memory that bad?" he mocked him, rudely.

"I'm not in the mood for this, so take a hike." He retorted, lying down on the chaise longue again and closing his eyes.

Another kick knocked him into the floor.

"Get up, although I agree with the redheaded, that you don't deserve a second chance, it's my job, and I always do my job." He shouted, sounding like damn staff argent, making his head ache so much it seemed to be ready to explode.

"Ok, let's get over it. I want to get back to sleep in peace." He stammered through gritted teeth, getting up and facing the man.

"Do you really believe you'll be able to have another night of peaceful sleep in your life?" the other man asked mocking him. *"Tell me, did you father find peace when your mother gave up on him?"*

"Don't mention my father." He threatened, closing his hands into tight fists.

"Or what? I'll mention him as much as I want, because he's the one to blame for you being the cold, arrogant badass you are." The spirit replied. *"His coldness, his indifference was the responsible for your mother's departure. She got tired of being miserable, of feeling less important than a rug."*

"She left because she didn't love us." Alec shouted.

"*Of course she did, especially you. But you turned your back on her, too stubborn to listen to her. And you're doing the same again. You know why Katherine's words sounded too familiar to you? Because you heard them on your mother's mouth fourteen years ago, the day she left your father.*"

Alec rubbed his face, controlling his urgent desire to knock out the man in front of him. He didn't want to hear this, he didn't want to accept the truth in his words, because he didn't want to admit he had just destroyed the best thing that had ever happened in his life.

"*Let's take a look at the brilliant future you have assured yourself.*" *The man said, taking him by his elbow and throwing him into a wild swirl that almost made him throw up, when they finally came to a stop.*

They were at the club. The place had the usual crowd, but seated at a table, old, with a bitter grin on his face was a man that he recognized as himself. He was alone, and looking at him he was sure he had been alone for a long time.

"*Look at you!*" *the spirit's voice sounded scornful.* "*You don't even bother trying to find someone to warm your bed for a few hours. You know it's useless. You're so bitter no one even tries to talk to you. You no longer have friends and your employees only stick around you the minimum time possible."*

Alec crossed his arms over his chest and tightened his lips, and didn't utter a single word.

"Now, let's take a look a James' future. According to you, he must be as miserable as you." The spirit said, taking him to another spin. They arrived to James's house. It was Christmas, and the house was decorated with colorful lights and even a huge Santa's sleigh, over the roof. The main door opened up and an older James came out dragging an older Hannah outside.

"See, this year there are no flaws." He was saying to a mesmerized Hannah, holding her close to his chest.

"Oh, Sir, it's so beautiful. The kids will love it!" she whispered, delighted.

"The only one that matters for me is you, pet. You're the owner of my heart, and the keeper of my soul." He said between kisses.

"Oh, yes, I can see it clearly. The man couldn't be more miserable." the spirit said, contemptuous. "The woman, you thought only wanted him for his money, is still beside him, thirty years later, and still loves him as much as she did on day one."

"I'm happy for him." Alec said coldly. And he was, but he was also sorry for losing his friend, for

not believing in him. At the end, he seemed to be a better judge of character than he was.

The spirit shook his head with despair. "No wonder you ended up alone. A dead fish has more emotions than you." He retorted. "Let's take a look at the woman you destroyed a few hours ago." He added, taking him inside the turmoil again.

They landed on a grave yard, in front of a recent grave, still bearing no name.

"She died?" Alec turned to the spirit, grabbing him by the lapels of the jacket he was wearing, his voice hoarse from the bulge on his throat, and the crashing weight in his chest.

"Why do you care? After all she was just a fuck toy to you. I'm sure that by now, you don't even remember her." The punch landed on his face throwing him a couple of feet away. The spirit slowly got up, rubbing his chin. "I'm just using your own words to describe her."

"Shut up. Just shut up." Alec threatened. "Where is she? What happened to her?" the dream didn't look like a dream anymore, and desperation was lodging in him like a weed.

"Don't worry, she doesn't lie there. That's the grave of her dreams and hopes." The spirit admitted with a sneering smile. "She resigned to BDSM, and never found someone to share her life

with. She dedicates her life to her work." He made Alec turn around in time to see Katherine strolling through the park near her house. She looked older, but she still had the power to warm his heart, and arouse his body. She still looked amazing.

"Are you done?" he asked the spirit, turning to face him.

"I just have a few questions for you: is saving your heart from a remote possibility of getting hurt worth the price of losing her? Is your stubbornness worth losing the love and respect of a man you care for, more than if he was your brother? Is your misdirected loyalty to your father worth losing the opportunity to fix things with your mother and enjoying her last years?" every word felt like a dagger directed to his heart.

"What do you want from me? To admit that I screwed everything? Yes, I did. I let fear from getting hurt to lead my actions. But now it's too late!" he shouted, his words pouring all his pain and regret.

The spirit led him through an even wilder swirl to make him end up back in his study. This time it was impossible to Alec to keep the contents of his stomach and he was only able to reach for the paper bin next to his desk, before he threw up violently. He had drunk way too much.

"Feeling better now?" the man asked, mocking him.

Alec looked up to him, with a murderer shine in his eyes. "I'm sure you've done your job, so get lost." He got up and faced the other man.

"All this time you've missed the point to these visits. We haven't gone through all this trouble just to rub your mistakes in your nose. Someone up there thinks you deserve another chance to rectify, to change your life." The spirit pointed out. "The future isn't written yet, but only you can change it, only you can make it different. On his visit to you, your father asked you to open your heart and mind, to avoid committing the mistakes he committed."

Alec looked at him, still filled with doubts, still afraid.

"Man, are you sure you're a Master? Because you resemble more to a chicken to me. Man up, damn it." The man poked him, furious.

Alec lunged at the other man, but only managed to land on the floor, after the spirit disappeared into thin air, the echo of his laughter lingering behind him.

Chapter Twenty Four

Alec got up and walked to the window. This time he wasn't able to convince himself that it all had been just a dream.

He was wide awake, and for the first time in years he let hope to creep back to his heart and light up a tiny light.

At least he had to try. And he was starting from the beginning.

He grabbed his cell phone and called Jack.

"I need a favor."

"You still owe me one from last time." The other man laughed.

"I'll pay them, no matter what."

"Wow that must be big."

"Can you please send me my mother's address?" though he had refused to talk to her ever since the day she left, he had always had someone checking on her for him, making sure she didn't need anything.

"On its way. But that's not the favor you want." Jack could read him well. They had known each other for years now, and as they say, it takes a loner to know one.

"When you looked for Katherine for me, did you get a lot of information about her?"

"You know me, thorough should be my second name." Jack admitted. He always digs all he could on everyone. "I have a whole file on her, but it's a very boring one."

"Do you know where her parents live?"

"Of course. Sending that information too. Need company?"

"Thank you, I need to do this on my own." Alec answered, rubbing his face. He needed a shower first, though.

"As you wish."

"Wait, maybe there's a place I could use your assistance." Alec remembered Lucy, Katherine's best friend. He felt he owed her an apology.

"Just name it."

"I need to find Lucy, Katherine's best friend, and I'm sure I'll need moral support when I meet her."

"I'll send you her whereabouts as soon as I find them. We'll meet there."

"Perfect, Jack, thank you." He ended the call and went straight to the shower. He got dressed, packed a few clothes, hurriedly, and before he left, he went to her room to pick up her collars. Somehow, having them made him feel hopeful.

He grabbed his SUV from the garage and entered his mother's address to the GPS system. In less than thirty minutes he was parking his car in front of a small house. Its gardens looked beautiful despite the winter cold.

It took him a great deal of courage to hop out of the car and stand in the sidewalk. All of a sudden, the front door opened up and his mother came out, almost running towards him. She stopped a couple of steps away from him.

"Alec..." she whispered, and he could see in her eyes all the love, the hope and just how much she had missed him.

He closed the distance between them and took her in his arms, holding her tight to him, his nostrils being invaded by the familiar perfume of roses his mother had always worn.

"I'm sorry..." he started to say but his mother rested a finger over his lips.

"Let's not waste time in useless excuses or explanations. You're here now and that's all that matters." She dragged him inside the house, and they spent a next two hours updating the news of their lives. "Your friend Jack keeps me updated, actually. He seems to enjoy my chocolate cake, so we spend a nice time together." Her mother informed him.

"Jack comes personally?" that surprised him, but not as much as it should have.

"Yes, he has become a good friend."

"I'm glad to hear it, mom."

After a little while he said goodbye to his mother promising to come back soon, and headed to the address Jack had sent him.

He parked the car in front of a park, near a few office buildings. Jack was already there waiting for him.

"Thank you." Alec said when he met him at the entrance.

Jack seemed to know exactly what he meant, because he just shrugged. "She's having lunch at the park and she's alone."

"Let's go then."

The two men walked in silence until they found a lovely brunette sitting in a bench, eating a sandwich while talking over the phone with someone.

"I'll kill him for you. You just need to tell me where I can find him." She was saying when they stopped in front of her. She looked up, and her eyes shined in recognition. "Never mind, I'll call you later." She ended the call, setting the phone carefully inside her purse, and putting down her sandwich. "I must say you have guts." She said, staring directly at Alec.

"Before you kill me, can I convince you to listen to me fort a couple of minutes?" he asked, with a self-deprecating grin.

"Well, I always say everybody is entitled to their last words, so choose yours carefully." Her tone showed all the disdain she felt for him.

Jack, beside him, chuckled amused with the woman's belligerence, getting elbowed by Alec.

"Even if it takes me the rest of my life, I'm going to solve things with Katherine and I'll make her the happiest woman on earth." He told, exposing his heart. "But before I go up north to meet her, and beg her forgiveness, I thought I owed you an apology. I should have accepted you invitation on Thanks Giving, and only my stubbornness stopped me from doing it. I'm aware you're Katherine's best friend and a very important person in her life, and that's why I'm here."

Lucy looked at him in silence for a couple of minutes, and Alec could feel the tension between them as thick and heavy as it could be.

"You just bought yourself a temporary pardon on your sentence. Don't hurt her even more or I swear I'll make sure your life is a living hell." She finally said, her arms crossed over her chest.

"Thank you, I promise I'll only live to make her happy." He vowed. "I know I don't deserve your favor, but can I ask you something? Don't tell her I'm going there. I don't want her to run away from me."

"I won't, but not for you, for her, so don't make me regret it." She warned him.

"I assure you I won't." he promised her, planting a smacking kiss on her cheeks, and leaving the park.

"Wow, that's quite a little caldron." James whistled surprised.

"You have to meet Katherine. I compared her with Katherine from *Taming the Shrew*, even before I knew her name was Katherine." Alec told his friend with a nostalgic smile. Despite his words to Lucy he feared his meeting with

Katherine. He was afraid he had been able to kill any feelings she might have had for him, but he had one more thing to do before he went to meet her. He had to find James and Hannah. "Thank you for coming with me. You can tab that as body guard work." He chuckled, but deep inside he knew Lucy had all the right in the world to be mad at him.

"Always a pleasure working for you." Jack said saying good bye.

Alec looked at his watch. It was almost five o'clock in the afternoon. James should be about to get home, so he decided to wait for him at his place. He drove there and waited parked in front of the house.

When he saw his car pulling in his drive way he hopped out of his car and strode to meet him before he entered the house.

"James." He called him when he got close enough.

The other man stopped and turned around surprised. When he confirmed it really was Alec walking towards him, his expression changed and he crossed his arms over his chest.

"This is a surprise. What happened? Did I leave any debt at the club?" he asked in an icy tone.

"What?" Alec asked, a bit lost. "No, I'm not here to talk about the club." He clarified.

"Then I can't think of any other reason to explain your presence in my house."

Alec could sense all the pain James had in storage, through each of his words. "I'm aware that I lost all rights to visit you in your house, and I can't say I blame you. I'm leaving up north to spend Christmas, but I couldn't leave without apologizing to you and Hannah." He explained, decided to put his heart out to convince James he was sincere. "Ever since my mother left my father, and a few other women left me, I tagged all women as gold diggers, unworthy of trust and obviously undeserving of love. Hannah wasn't the exception, and if you add that to the fact I feared I would lose your friendship, she became the target of all my hatred." He sighed, and moved uncomfortable. He wasn't used to expose his feelings that way and he was having a hard time doing it. Add that to James' tense silence, and he was more than ready to flee the place. "I realized I was acting as real bastard and that you two really love each other."

James snorted. "What made you have this sudden epiphany?"

"Falling in love with my other half, the keeper of my soul." He answered, putting into words for the first time his feelings for Katherine. "Listen, I don't expect you to forgive me for all the bad times I made you go through. I just wanted to say I'm sorry, and that my club will always welcome you and your wife. And, I'm really happy for your baby."

"Since I wasn't the most aggravated person in all this, I believe you should apologize as well to Hannah." James replied, walking towards the door without waiting for Alec's answer.

He opened the door and Hannah was waiting for them a few feet from the door, obviously ready to receive her master, but without knowing how to act in presence of Alec.

"Hannah, Alec wants to talk to you, and I decided to let him do it." James explained his wife.

Hannah looked at Alec, all her rage shining in her eyes. "I have no idea what he might want to say to me, Sir."

"Like I already told James I just want to apologize to both of you for my past behavior. I know I hurt you both and I'll never be able to show you two just how sorry I am." He said, locking his eyes in hers, letting his soul show itself to her. He wanted to make sure they couldn't doubt he was been truthful.

"Do we owe this change of heart to your new submissive?" she asked, with a different shine in her eyes.

"Yes, she made me realize just how fucked up I've been most of my life." He recognized. "I know I was especially rude with you, and I'm sorry for that. I just wanted you to know that." He added. "I won't take more of your time. I wish you a Merry Christmas, and I hope to see you back at the club, whenever you feel like going back."

"Can't you stay for dinner?" Hannah asked, and Alec looked at her surprised and then looked at James. His friend had his usual broad smile captured in his face.

"I would love to, believe me, but I want to get to Katherine tonight." And he was being honest. Seeing James back to his old self had taken a huge weight from his chest. "If I manage to get her back, we'll be celebrating New Year's Eve and I would love to see you guys there."

"I'm sure you'll get her back. Just show her your heart." Hannah, advised him and with a self-deprecating smile he nodded.

He said goodbye and left.

Chapter Twenty Five

Once in his car he set the GPS with the address Jack had sent him and started his journey.

It was a long ride, and he got rain and even snow on the way, but he drove nonstop. He wanted to get there and feel at least closer to her.

He arrived to her home town past ten o'clock. Though he knew it was too late to go knocking at their door, he drove his car straight there. The house was decorated with Christmas lights all over, and there was light in all the windows of the ground floor, and you could see several people wandering from one room to another. It looked like they really took the holidays seriously.

Unwilling to ruin their night he started the car to go find a hotel to spend the night, when the main door opened up and she came out, alone, closing the door behind her.

It was cold outside, it had snowed earlier and you could still see some of the snow on people's gardens, but she came out just wearing a light sweater. She sat in a swing on the porch, and hid her face on her hands.

Even from a certain distance he could feel the pain in her.

Before he could think much about it, he turned off the car and hopped out of it. He needed to make her pain go away, even if it meant to replace it with rage.

He walked silently to where she was and with every step he took, her sobs sounded louder. He knelt in front of her.

"Please don't cry, girl." He whispered, resting his hands on her knees.

She uncovered her face and looked at him astonished.

"You... what are you doing here?" she whispered as well, as if she wasn't sure he was real.

"I know you told me to stay out of your life, but I can't, I just don't know how to live without you anymore." He confessed, holding her cold hands in his.

"Toys are easily replaced. You didn't look long enough." She retorted, pushing her hands out of his. "Please leave, I don't want my family to see you here." She added, getting up.

He lowered his head but nodded. He knew it was late but he hadn't been able to resist the sight of her.

"I'll leave, but I'll come back tomorrow, and the day after tomorrow and the days it takes me to gain your forgiveness." He warned her, getting up, restraining the strong desire to hold her in his arms and never let go.

"There's nothing to forgive. Actually, I appreciated your honesty. It stopped me from wasting any more time waiting on an impossible dream." Her reply was filled with self-scorn, as she hugged herself, rubbing her arms.

"That morning I was anything but honest. I was a coward, a liar, an arrogant bastard... all you want to call me, but not honest, because not even a single word I uttered carried any truth in it." He admitted, but he knew she didn't believe him. Gently, he wiped a tear from her cheek, feeling her shudder under his touch. "You should go in, it's too cold out here. But, know this, I won't give up. I've already wasted too much time of my life being afraid of my feelings."

"Feelings? Do you even know the meaning of that word, *Alec*?" she asked, emphasizing his name to let him know he no longer was her Master. That simple act hurt like stab to his heart, but he knew he deserved it.

"I learned it in the past twenty four hours and I will not forget it again."

"I'm glad for you, but I won't go through this again. I've wasted too many tears over you, I'm not doing it again." Her pain was clear in every word.

"I know I don't deserve another chance, but I just can't give up."

"What do I have to do to convince you I won't change my mind?"

"Convince me I've killed any feelings you might have felt for me and I'll leave you alone." He gave her the weapon able to destroy him, but the stubborn hope lit on his heart refused to believe she was going to be able to use it.

She looked at him for a few moments and seemed to make a decision.

"Wait here." She entered the house and was away for a few minutes. When she came back, she was wearing a coat and carried her purse. "Have you checked in at the hotel?"

"Not yet, I was about to look for it when I saw you come out earlier."

"I'll take you there and then we can talk."

They drove off in his car and only a couple of minutes later they were parking the SUV in the hotel's parking lot. He checked in and she followed him to his room. She was too quiet for his likings and that worried him. She had always been feisty, foulmouthed and he had always loved that in her. This quiet Katherine worried him.

Once they reached his bedroom, she walked to the window and stared outside for a while, before she turned to meet his gaze. "Why did you come after me again?"

"I finally realized what I had been doing to myself for the past fourteen years..." he explained all to her. He told her about his mother, his father, about Rose and all his failed relationships and the way they all had contributed to make him a mistrustful, arrogant bastard. "You were able to shake the pillars of my high dais ever since the moment you almost knocked me to the ground on the dark street. All my convictions started to crumble little by little every time we were together. The night you left me for the first time, the connection between us was so strong, it overwhelmed me and scared the hell out of me. I wasn't ready for that, for that kind of emotional intensity and I acted as I knew best: like a cruel asshole."

She snorted but didn't say a word.

He considered telling her about the spirits' visit, but he could tell she was reluctant to believe him. Adding that part of the story would probably blow his chances with her. "When I realized I had sent you away after an intense rope scene and how dangerous the drop can be, I panicked and tried to find you and when I did, relief and rage mixed and none of what I had planned to tell you came out of my mouth. Despite that, somehow I managed to get you back." He rubbed his face, feeling the tiredness of the last twenty four hours start to affect him. "The time you lived with me is the happiest I recall living. I had never felt so happy, so fulfilled in my entire life. Going home acquired a new meaning, because it meant I would find you there."

"How can you say all that when you said I was nothing more than a good fucking toy?" she finally broke her silence but her words were filled of bitterness and self-disdain. "I doubt you can experience warm feelings over a person so it's kind of hard to believe you were happy living with a toy."

"Those words will haunt me for the rest of my life." He accepted taking a step closer to her, just to see her take a step back. "Katherine, I've never considered any of my submissives a toy, I certainly would never consider you. You have been special to me since the first moment."

"Well I'm sorry but I find that hard to believe. You kept me away from your life, you made me sleep alone, you never introduced me to any of your friends, you never took me out on a date, you refused to meet my friends and finally you refused to meet my family, even though I had told you how important that was to me." She enounced all his misdeeds.

"I was afraid, I didn't want to share you with anyone. Every time I took you to the club I was afraid you might meet someone that would convince you, you were better off without me."

"And you thought that by insulting me you would keep me?" her ironic disbelief hurt him.

"Of course not, but I tend to defend myself when I feel at bay."

His answer only made angrier. "I wasn't trying to put at bay, Alec, I just wanted to make you part of all my life."

"I know, and now I understand that, and that's why I'm here. To ask you to forgive me." He admitted taking another step closer to her just to see her take another step back.

"Very well, I forgive you. I understand you had trusting issues, and that you solved them somehow. That makes me happy for you, and I wish you all the luck in the world."

"But...?"

"You have hurt me too much for me to trust you again. I admit we lived amazing moments but I'm sure you'll find someone more suitable for you."

"I don't want anybody else." He assured her.

"Why? And taking the risk of being repetitive I'll ask you again: What am I to you?" she asked bracing herself.

"I heard the description a friend made of his wife and I believe it fits perfectly to what you are to me: you are the owner of my heart and the keeper of my soul. I love you more than life itself."

Katherine looked at him wanting to believe his words so much but too afraid.

"Would you still love me if I told I don't love you?" she asked, deciding to put his love to test, using his past experiences.

He visibly cringed before answering. "My love for you doesn't depend on either you love me or not."

She gathered all her inner strength before she proceeded.

"The truth is I really enjoyed living with you, having all I might need and working only when I want, having a luxurious life... would you accept me back in your house even if I don't love you?"

Her words felt like daggers and he looked at her. Could she be telling the truth? That she would be with him just for what he could give her? He filtered all the time she had been with him and he had never seen anything that might hint that she was a material person. She had never asked him anything material. So this is was a test and he had to approve it.

"I would take back under any condition. My love would be enough for both of us." He finally answered, with a resolved expression in his face.

"Any condition? You should be careful with what you say, I might take your word for it."

"Any condition, Katherine, I would trust my whole life to you."

"Aren't you afraid I might abuse of the power you're giving me?"

"No, not you."

"But I don't love you."

"Even so, it's not in you to hurt other people on purpose."

"How can I trust this change of hearts of yours?" she asked, tears rolling down her cheeks.

"I didn't change, girl, think about it. When did I treat you like an object? Remember all the amazing moments we lived together." He closed the distance between them, not stopping until he had her in his arms. "I've always treated you like what you really are to me: the most precious treasure I've ever had." He wiped the tears from her face. "My stupid fears made me lie to you and I know I hurt you, deeply with my words. But I love you, and life without you isn't worth living." He cuddled her face with his hands and kissed her deeply.

She started crying out loud and he held her tight in his arms until she calmed down again.

"I love you so much…" she murmured against his chest.

A wave of relief rushed through his body and he hugged her tighter.

"I love you too, girl. And this time we'll do things right: I'll meet your family and ask your father permission to marry you." She chuckled and hugged him back.

"I would love that Master."

That word back in her mouth felt wonderfully and he promised himself he was going to cherish her like he had never done in his life.

He carried her in his arms towards the bed and they spent the rest of the night recovering the lost time

She shouldn't have accepted to join Mark that night at the club. The look in his eyes, when he asked her to, had sent a shudder down her spine, and ever since that moment she had felt nervous and jumpy. What could he possibly have in mind for that night?

So far he had made her experience so much that sometimes, her mind seemed to need time to process it all.

But nothing could keep her from going and she knew it.

She arrived at the club and Sally informed her that he was already in. She looked around the reception room and for her surprise, she found Emily there.

She felt the blood rushing to her face as she approached her friend.

"Emily!" she stammered. "What are you doing here?"

Her friend smiled, patting the seat next to her on the couch. Rose walked towards her and sat next to her.

"I'm guessing the same thing you are." she answered, teasingly. "Are you here to meet Mark?"

"Yes, we are sort of dating…?" she said, unable to describe her relationship with the man, in a more accurate way.

"It was obvious that first night you two had something going on, Rose." Emily interrupted her. "And this isn't the first time he brings you back here, right?"

"No, but I still get so nervous sometimes I think I'll pass out!" Rose said, wringing her hands. "What about you? Are you meeting Damian?" she asked, changing the subject.

"Yes, I am, but he is running a bit late tonight." Her friend answered.

"Oh!" Rose sighed, still obviously nervous. "I shouldn't have come, this is insane, I knew it, but he was so convincing…" she blurted out.

"Don't you want to be with him? Did he coerce you in anyway?" Emily asked her, suddenly worried.

"No!" Rose almost shouted. "It's just I don't seem to be able to handle this guy, I mean…" she ran her fingers nervously, through the leather 'play collar' as he called it, that she was wearing on her neck.

"I know what you mean." Emily agreed.

"Can you go in with me? I would feel so much more comfortable with you there." She asked Emily. Having her friend next to her would make her feel so much better.

Emily seemed to hesitate.

"Please?" Rose insisted, grabbing her friend's hands.

"Sally, do you think it would be ok if I go in with my friend and wait for Master Damian there with her and Master Mark?" Emily turned to ask the other woman.

"Well, I guess. I'll warn Master Damian where he can find you." Sally said, smiling.

Rose filled up her forms quickly and soon they were both in the main room.

"Can you see Mark?" Rose asked Emily, looking around impatiently. The place was crowded and it was a bit hard to find someone in it.

"Didn't you settle a meeting place?" Emily asked her.

"I didn't think I would need it." Rose answered her, furious with herself for not thinking of that, and furious with Mark for not being there, even if that was a bit illogical.

"Let's walk around the room, to see if we can spot him." Emily suggested and they walked around the room with no luck.

"I don't understand! Sally told me he was already here. I know I arrived a bit sooner than expected, but, where the hell can he be?" Rose said, stamping her foot on the floor, frustrated.

"Why don't we sit at a table and wait there? Maybe he is in one of the dungeons and won't come up until your settled hour." Emily suggested her, smiling amused.

"Yes, maybe you are right. Why don't you go ahead and find us a table? I need to use the ladies room first." The nervousness always affected her bladder.

"Ok, but please don't take too long." Emily said.

"I won't." Rose promised and headed to the ladies room. She did what she had to do and came out only a couple of minutes later. She still had fifteen minutes to wait for Mark.

She walked to the tables' area but Emily was nowhere to be found.

Rose looked around, looking for her, but she couldn't find her.

Shrugging, she assumed Damian had arrived and that she had left with him.

At that moment, she felt a shiver run down her spine and she quickly turned around just to find Mark standing a few steps away from her, his strong arms crossed over his chest. He was wearing black leather pants and vest and he looked like a damn Viking that had just walked out of his boat, ready to raid the peasant's village. His blue eyes had this dangerous glow that was able to forget everything else around them.

"Good evening, little rose." He said, with a devious smile. "Are you ready for me?" he asked, his tone showing he didn't expect anything other than a 'yes, master'.

"Good evening, Master Mark. Actually, I was heading to the bar for a drink, after all, it's still early." She answered, determined to poke him.

He smiled, and she had the infuriating sensation that he could read her like an open book.

"Then I'll join you. I could use a glass of cold water." He said, taking her by her arm and guiding her towards the bar. He ordered for both of them, and they lingered there, enjoying their cold beverages.

They didn't have much time there when Damian approached them.

"Mark!" he said as he reached his friend. "Where's Emily?"

"She's not with you?" Rose asked, stepping up, to face him.

"Of course not, I'm just arriving!" Damian almost shouted. "Where is she?"

Rose lost all color from her cheeks, as she realized Emily was missing.

"She came in with me, and I left her alone for a few minutes while I went to the ladies room. She was supposed to wait for me at a table, but when I came out she wasn't anywhere to be seen, so I assumed you had arrived and that she was with you." She explained to both men.

"Damn!" Damian swore, looking worried and furious at the same time.

"She wasn't wearing your collar?" Mark asked, understanding the possibilities.

"No! I was going to talk to her about that today! Damn!" Damian rubbed his hand over his face. "Do we have too many guests around today?" he asked Mark.

"Yes, half a dozen men, from Russia, that came with the Russian consul." Mark answered, expressing the same worry as Damian.

"Shit! Please gather a few monitors and make them look for her. She is reddish, with green eyes and a very white skin." He shouted the orders as he started running towards the stairs that led to the dungeons.

Mark turned around to face Rose.

"Wait here for me! Don't move a single muscle, not even to go to the ladies room." Mark's order was clear and raw. He was furious and worried, and that wasn't a good combination.

He ran after Damian and Rose watched him disappear worried for Emily. It wasn't like her to disappear like that.

She stood there watching the seconds ran by on her watch, looking around, wanting to go look for her friend, but paralyzed by Mark's words. He would kill her if he returned and she wasn't there. He didn't need more trouble right now.

So, she stood there, bouncing from one foot to the other, looking desperately around and following the slow advance of the watch.

Finally, she saw Mark with other monitors walking a man to the exit. She took a step to go meet him, just to take it back. She crossed her arms tight around her chest, even more worried. A few minutes later she saw Damian coming out of the hall way with Emily and this time she had to make a huge effort not to run towards her friend. She watched them leave the club, feeling helpless.

Mark soon returned to where she was. His face didn't inspire anything good. He was furious and she guessed good part of it was directed at her.

He grabbed her by her arm and almost dragged her to the upper floor, to one of the private rooms.

He chose one that looked like a small medieval dungeon, and she felt shivers ran down her spine. That didn't look good for her.

"Assume your position." Were his first words to her and she didn't doubt obeying.

"Yes, Master." She fell to her knees, her buttocks resting over her ankles, hands behind her back and her head down.

He stood in front of her and raised her chin with one of his fingers.

"What role did you play in this situation?" his tone was harsh and cold like a winter's day.

"I met Emily at the entrance and asked her to accompany me inside, Master." She answered. "I didn't notice she wasn't wearing a collar, so I left her alone for just a couple of minutes while I went to the ladies room."

"She was grabbed by a foreign guest and he was about to torture her and god knows what else." He informed, his words spewing rage. "He completely ignored her cries for help and her safe word."

"Oh, god. She didn't want to come in, but I insisted, and I was so nervous she ended up accepting." Rose stammered, almost speaking for herself.

"So you induced her to disobey her Dom." He concluded.

"I didn't know she had been told to stay there." She replied, protesting for the unfair comment.

"Don't you think you should have known better? After all I had explained in great detail the dangers of wandering alone and uncollared through the club." His tone was even colder and she shuddered.

"Yes, Master, I should have known better." And she did. When she asked Emily to enter the main room with her, she should have checked if she had a collar on, and she hadn't. And if that wasn't enough, she had left her alone. "I'm terribly sorry." She added, a silent tear running down from the corner of her eye.

"You will be." He said, and his menacing tone made her close her eyes, not scared, but yes concerned. "The minute you made her enter the club with you, she became your responsibility and you neglected that.

"Yes Master." She admitted the weight of what might have happened, downing on her. Her nervousness had taken the best of her and she had missed important things.

"What should I do to you now, little rose?" he asked, his tone still harsh, but the rage was gone.

His question, though, made her sob. Was he giving up on her? She knew she had been complaining that she didn't know how to handle him, but if one thing she had clear, was that she didn't want to lose him. Not yet.

It was dark when I woke up and I was alone with my thoughts. Time was beginning to become meaningless, and I had no idea if it was day or night, nor did I care. Why did it matter? It wouldn't make me any less of his slave.

I let my mind drift to what my days used to be like. I thought about what I used to do each day at work and I could almost smell the coffee I would have each morning at my desk, when I first got into the office.

My mind began to wander from the life I used to have to what happened earlier. There was a burning sensation from the tattoo. I can't believe he branded me like I was his property. It was still bandaged but I didn't need to see the ink on my wrist to remember what happened.

I heard Devlin in the kitchen and realized I wasn't handcuffed to the bed. This was the first time I had woke up untethered. I thought about trying to make a run for it, but quickly put that thought out of my head. I wouldn't make it to the front door before he caught me and I still hadn't figured out where the stupid fire escape even was, if there even was one. Surely there had to be one. Don't all hi-rise buildings have to have them?

The more I thought about everything, the angrier I became. This tattoo was the final straw. I decided that I'd had enough and went into the kitchen to confront him.

"I'm not doing this anymore Devlin."

He leaned against the counter and smirked.

"You've kidnapped me, held me hostage, refused to let me wear clothes, beat me repeatedly, made me crawl around on all fours like I was an animal and you won't even let me go potty with the bathroom door locked and now you've marred my body with this tattoo."

I lifted my wrist and pointed to the bandage.

"What are you going to do next, get out a cattle iron and brand my ass?"

He didn't respond. He just kept looking at me with that smirk on his face.

"I can't even sleep like a normal person at night because you insist on handcuffing me to the bed. I'm not doing this anymore. I've had enough. I want to go home. You've had your fun but enough is enough. I'm not your pet. I'm a human being and I have rights. You can't treat me like this."

He just kept grinning at me and let me continue on with my rant. He didn't even appear to be angry with me, seeming almost amused by my outburst.

"Well, say something!" I demanded.

"Aren't we feeling a little spunky today?"

"If you think I'm going to answer you 'Yes, Master' you've lost your mind. I'm done with all of that. I want to go home Devlin. I'm serious. Take me home right this minute!"

I turned with my back to him, not wanting to let him see me tear up. And then I felt him. He came up behind me and a sensation unlike any I had felt before tore through me. I couldn't feel him but I knew he was near me. The pull was beyond my control.

There was something delusional about these thoughts I kept having about him. This man is forcing my sanity to fly out the window and I couldn't for the life of me explain why. I enjoyed being the focus of his attention, and I enjoyed the way he took care of me yet at the same time, I knew that was wrong. I knew I shouldn't care anything about this man. This is my abductor, not a potential husband.

Being around Devlin had a strange effect on me, and I couldn't understand it. I mean yes he was a beautiful man -- that goes without saying, but I had been around attractive men before. It's not like I lived in a cave all of my life. But this was more and I couldn't quite put my finger on what it was about him that was beyond the normal realm of appealing. Why was I so drawn to him even after the way he has treated me?

For the last year, any time he was anywhere near me my brain would just shut down and my body would tingle with desire. A year of this unexplainable pull towards him, to have it all end up like this?

I remembered his touch, and a chill ran up my spine. How crazy am I to get turned on just by the memory of him touching me? What is wrong with me? God, I even loved the way he woke me up each morning, with his deep masculine voice. I really did love the way he said "Good morning." Then again, I loved the way he said most things. His voice alone could drive me over the edge.

"Are you finished?" he murmured from behind me.

I froze. His words hit me like a slap to the face. Am I finished? Seriously? That's all he had to say to me?

"Why are you doing this to me?" I asked, as I turned to face him.

He didn't answer my question. Instead he took me by the hand and led me into a room I hadn't seen before. He drenched my body in baby oil, taking his time to rub it in thoroughly, making my skin slick.

"This will help you not to get rope burns."

I didn't know what he meant but it felt so good having his hands all over my body, I didn't stop to give it much thought.

When he was done rubbing the baby oil in, he had me straddle a chair and then secured my legs far apart, keeping them in place with a thick rope. He handcuffed my hands behind my back and then put a ball gag in my mouth.

Now it didn't matter what he did to me, because I couldn't move or scream for help. I was scared. Maybe I shouldn't have had my little outburst after all.

"Your life is no longer your own. Your body belongs to me. I told you on that first day here, my word is law. You are my property, my slave. You will learn to obey me. You will learn to submit."

He smacked my upper thigh with a leather riding crop. It stung. He hit my other thigh, then my stomach, each of my breasts and then my pussy. The pain from that stroke was unimaginable. I cried out but the ball gag prevented any sound from being heard. Luckily he didn't hit my pussy but the one time. The other strokes were focused mostly on my upper thighs and stomach, with each of my breasts getting struck a few times as well.

I don't know how long this went on, it could have been twenty strokes or two hundred. All I knew for sure was that my body was bright red and swollen from being struck repeatedly with the riding crop.

I knew what he was doing. He was breaking me down so that he could build me back up. I got it. The military does the same thing. That's what basic training was all about. But even knowing what he was doing, didn't make the pain he inflicted any easier to bare.

The red slashes and welts covered practically all of my body. I began to grow woozy and started to pass out from the pain. It was all just too much to take. I couldn't handle it anymore.

When I woke up I was handcuffed to the bed again, alone in the dark. Tears began streaming down my cheeks, my voice quaking in terror, as I let out a pitiful cry.

My body ached from the lashes that had bitten into my bare flesh and I was feeling sick to my stomach, I felt like I might throw up but I couldn't move. If I was going to get sick, I would have to lay there in it for God only knows how long, until he came in to check on me and let me clean myself up. If he let me clean myself up. He was a sadistic bastard, for all I knew, he would make me lay in my own vomit to punish me for getting sick in the first place.

I did my best to keep from throwing up and eventually, when I stopped crying he came into the bedroom. He released me from the cuffs and helped me sit up and gently brushed the hair out of my eyes.

With him he had a bowl of ice cold water and some strips of linen which he dipped into the freezing water and lightly placed on my skin. The coolness of the cloth felt good and helped to sooth the welts on my body. I laid perfectly still as he cared for my wounds.

"That's a good girl," he soothed.

While he was caring for me, I must have fallen back asleep. I don't know how long I was out but when I woke up I could see the sun shining through the window and knew it was a new day.

I could smell the scent of fresh bacon and heard my stomach growl and soon after Devlin entered the room with a tray in hand. For breakfast today he made scrambled eggs, bacon, toast with strawberry jelly and a glass of orange juice.

I tried to use my one free hand to prop myself up, but it hurt too much to move. I grimaced and he rushed to my side, setting the tray of food down and removed my handcuffs.

"Good morning," he said as he helped me sit all the way up.

"I need to go to the restroom. Do you think you can help me get up?"

He gave me a stern look. "Please Master, I don't think I can get out of bed without your help."

He smiled down at me and gently helped me get out of bed. As soon as I stood up I fell to the floor. The pain was so intense, I couldn't stand up on my own. He picked me up off of the floor and carried me to the bathroom, sitting me down on the toilet. I was humiliated at having him there while I relieved myself but what else could I do? I couldn't walk without him. After I finished he helped me wash my hands and face and then carried me back to bed and fed me breakfast.

He was so tender and loving with me and for just a moment it was easy to imagine having a great life with him. That is, this version of him. I liked him liked this. I liked having him lavish me with affection and attention. This was the Devlin that I was first attracted to. He had a sensitive loving heart and lively spirit that drew everyone to him. If only this Devlin would stay around all the time.

After breakfast Devlin ran me a warm bath that he had filled with Epsom salt to help my wounds heal and the swelling go down. When we were done he carried me back to bed and rubbed scented oils into my body. It was relaxing and before long I was asleep yet again. I had read once that when you are not feeling well your body uses sleep to help recover. As much as I was sleeping lately, I supposed my body's recovery system must have been in hyper-drive.

After a few days of extensive bed rest and tender, loving care from Devlin I finally started to feel almost human again. Devlin informed me that he had to go into work for a few hours. I felt almost panicked at hearing that he would be leaving me alone and it must have shown on my face.

"It's okay," he said soothingly as he patted my leg. "I'll be back before you know it. Do you want to watch some television while I am away?"

"I would. Thank you Master."

This was the first time he was going to trust me out of bed while he was away. There wouldn't however be a chance for me to escape because he secured me to a chair in the living room. I had one hand free but one hand and both legs were chained.

I flipped mindlessly through the channels until I happened upon a re-run of one of the Twilight movies. I've seen them all before, several times before, but nothing else was on so I watched it again.

When the movie ended I started flipping channels again and happened upon a skin flick, one of the 'Cinemax After Dark' type movies about two girls who were in love with the same guy but decided to get back at him for cheating on them both by dating each other.

Caught up in the show, I didn't hear the noise of the door opening before it was too late and Devlin entered the penthouse.

"Well, well. What do we have here?" He asked, as he came in and looked at what was on the television.

I scrambled to turn it off but it was too late. He had already seen what was on the screen.

"It's not what you think."

"What is it then? Are you telling me you don't have some secret desire to be with another girl?"

Get your Kindle copy of Submission Today

Or get the Audio Book

Top Customer Reviews

4 of 5 people found the following review helpful
⭐⭐⭐⭐⭐ **A Steamy Office Romance**
By Devon on May 25, 2015
Format: Kindle Edition · Verified Purchase

I was looking for a book to keep me entertained and excited, and I found that and more with "Submission" by Veronica Cane. I am not usually into BDSM but this feels different. It was a bit raunchy but that is what made it interesting. Following Mary Elizabeth through her exploration of her new sexual interests is what made the book interesting to read.

Do not read this if you don't want your glasses to get all fogged up from the steam.

Comment   Was this review helpful to you?   Yes   No   Report abuse

1 of 1 people found the following review helpful
⭐⭐⭐⭐ **Kept you listening till the end**
By Luzmaria on October 17, 2015
Format: Audible Audio Edition

I listened to the audiobook version of this book.

I was caught off guard with the Dom - sub relationship. In my opinion it was not one. It was a dark book that I believe was supposed to be a master-slave relationship? The strangest thing about it though was that he just basically kidnapped her and told her she was now his slave and she just goes along with it? That left me confused as a reader and baffled as a woman. Was there some Stockholm Syndrome going on, low self esteem or a victim to previous abuse? I wish that was looked into more. With everything going on it left you wanting more to see what would happen. I didn't want to put it down. I really think because of that fact it was too much for me. I have a couple of friends who are into dark erotica as well and they both loved it. So it's all just personal preference.

I thought Jennifer Saucedo did an excellent job narrating this book. It's the best of her work that I've listened to from her.

Comment   Was this review helpful to you?   Yes   No   Report abuse

3 of 4 people found the following review helpful
⭐⭐⭐ **Frustrating!**
By A. cooke on July 21, 2015
Format: Kindle Edition

I thought I had already read this book at the beginning of the story. It seemed VERY familiar until I got to the abduction and then it became entirely different. I do enjoy good bdsm stories but I warned, this does NOT portray the bdsm lifestyle but slavery. Is it realistic? I have my doubts. Mary Elizabeth, our h, bemoans her situation but does nothing when she has the opportunity to escape. She loves Devlin, the H, even though he is cruel to her and not at all lovable. It's very apparent Mary Elizabeth has little, if any, self-respect and appreciates any crumbs of affection he is shown.

I probably would have enjoyed this story more if I wasn't so distracted by typos and the misuse of the English language. The words "I seen" were used repeatedly in place of the proper "I saw" and it drove me bonkers! Ms. Cane, please hire an editor for your next book. Your readers will thank you for it.

Comment   Was this review helpful to you?   Yes   No   Report abuse

1 of 1 people found the following review helpful
⭐⭐⭐⭐ **Wildly fun**
By Mouse3324 on October 9, 2015
Format: Kindle Edition

When I started writing it was to fulfill my childhood dream of being an author.

I've always been a storyteller and I've always loved romance. But it wasn't until recently that I found my true passion and hunger for the most sensual, erotic words and stories. I guess you could say I now write to fulfill my deepest adult fantasies. And I love every waking moment of it. That burning desire within me is satisfied with every zesty story that I write--and read. Fantasy, pleasure, awakening, stimulation--I can't get enough.

I hope you'll join me in my chase for the deepest sensual, romantic gratification possible.

Stay up to date with my books --or want to share with me the sexiest thing you've ever read--feel free to email me or join my newsletter to stay updated.

http://www.veronicacane.com

Printed in Great Britain
by Amazon

50138009R00149